Where's Lolly?

Stephen Henning

Copyright

Contents

Dedication

Thanks to my wife Rebecca for all her help, support and professional proofreading services. Thanks also to my mum, dad, brother and, in fact, my entire wonderful family – aunts, uncles, cousins, in-laws (FMIL) and nieces.

I love you all very much.

Chapter 1

I'm 16 years old and last night I cried for the first time in two years. That's a long time for most girls. The stupid ones will cry for any reason at all. Their mother doesn't understand them, a boy doesn't smile back, a dress doesn't fit, or a dog died. I've seen it all and it makes me sick.

Last night I cried because I was lonely. Simple as that.

I've discovered that it's surprisingly easy to feel lonely in London. I'm standing in the plaza looking up at One Canada Square in Canary Wharf, right at the heart of the city's financial district. It's lunchtime and all around me men and women in sharp suits are having urgent discussions about business deals and gossiping about colleagues. People are laughing, joking, maybe even flirting. They're all part of something. They all have each other. Then they'll go home to their families, friends, boyfriends, or girlfriends. I have nobody. Literally, nobody at all.

Actually, I think I *am* going to be sick. Anything will set me off at the moment. I should be ravenous but I still can't eat. Just looking at food makes me queasy. It seems like everybody here is holding a latte and a wrap, or they're sitting in the sunshine eating sushi out of plastic containers. On my way here from the station, I had to pass endless coffee shops, delicatessens, pubs and wine bars, all serving and boasting about their food.

You've probably come to the conclusion that I'm pregnant. Another 16-year-old schoolgirl who's been knocked up by a lothario-turned-scared-witless-classmate. I almost wish I was.

No, actually I'm ill. Don't worry, I'm not dying or anything, although for a while it felt as though I was. Somebody injected me with a very nasty drug a few days ago, which has taken away my most precious gifts and left me weak and vulnerable.

I need help, that's why I'm here. I need money and I need somewhere to stay for a while, until I recover – if I recover. I'm hoping I'll find what I need inside the huge glass skyscraper in front of me.

It's a cliché that I hear a lot of girls use, but my life is complicated right now. To add to my problems, the police, MI5 and probably some angry ex-boyfriends are looking for me. If they find me... well, I shudder to think what they will do to me.

I walk across the busy square, ignoring the hubbub of conversation about mergers, money and playing hard. I approach the steps leading up to the giant video screen that's showing 24/7 Interactive News bulletins. I hope they don't splash a photo of my face across the screen again like they did when I was in Liverpool Street Station, even though it was a really good picture. It was taken at a school fete. My hair was slightly shorter then. Shoulder length. The sun is behind me and I look almost blonde, even though I'm a brunette. In the photo, I'm wearing my old school uniform, but I make it look like something sported on the catwalk. That's one gift that no drug can ever take away from me.

I'm very pretty – I could easily be a model – I'm sexy and I know that guys look at me all the time. In fact I see a man looking at me now, stealing glances while he listens to the boring frump who's probably his boss as they hurry towards the shopping complex. I'm wearing a knee-length, white-lace dress. Not my favourite outfit, but it's cute on a sunny day, and I packed in a bit of a hurry. I do rather stand out among all the suits.

I guess I should try and change my appearance so as not to draw attention. I'm quite well known. Google 'Lolly Rosewood' and you'll find a picture of me with my father at a glitzy party, or lying on a beach with a now-forgotten ex.

I should wear something dull, dye my hair mousey, cut it short, that kind of thing. Make myself look boring. But I don't see why I should. I'm me! Lolly Rosewood doesn't change for anyone. I prefer to dazzle with my looks and hide in plain sight.

Uh-oh. The video *does* now show a picture of me and they're running the headline '*Where's Lolly?*' Very amusing! I like that one.

I quicken my step, just in case. Several bored workers stop to look up at the screen and gawp at my face. They're probably fantasizing about me, or maybe they're just thankful I'm not their daughter. I need to get inside quickly before anyone recognizes me. I don't have the strength to deal with an intervention.

The main entrance is about twenty metres away and a man is just exiting the building. He's in his fifties, he looks distinguished and he's wearing a nicely tailored suit. Daddy probably knows him. He's holding a sandwich and all of a sudden I'm swamped by a wave of nausea. My vision is blurry; please don't faint, please don't faint.

I keep going. I need to get out of the heat. It's 26 degrees Celsius today. Inside it will be air conditioned and I'll be ok.

I know you're dying to ask: why is everyone looking for me?

Well, my father is Sir Michael Rosewood. You've probably heard of him – and if you haven't then you're obviously stupid. Certainly everyone in Canary Wharf knows who he is. He's the most amazing, charismatic, powerful businessman in the country, probably the world. He's certainly one of the richest.

The media are saying, indeed they genuinely believe, that Daddy has retired to a secret island hideaway. They're saying that I didn't want to go and instead I disappeared from home and everyone is desperately worried about me. They're even suggesting I might have been kidnapped. Supposedly, Daddy has posted a reward of £100,000 leading to news of my safe rescue. The government think they are very clever, don't they?

The truth is that the authorities have kidnapped my father. They're treating him like a criminal. They're scared of him and they're scared of me. We're different, you see. We have special abilities. A boy I kind of know used to call our abilities 'superpowers'. I like that term. It's a bit geeky, but the boy is quite cute. I should hate him but I don't. His name is James and he made a big impression on me. It was he who injected me with the drug that has made me sick.

You see, I told you my life was complicated.

I'm ten metres from the sanctuary of the cool building, almost level with the distinguished gentleman, and he takes a bite of his sandwich. It's too much for me. I just about manage to prevent myself from actually being sick, but my legs give out underneath me.

The pavement is coming up at my face, but then I'm in a spin, and I think I can feel someone's arms around me. For a second it feels comforting, then I'm sucked into a tunnel of blackness.

Chapter 2

"Are you all right, dear? Are you feeling better?"

"Maybe she's diabetic? She could be having an episode. Does our insurance cover us?"

"Are you here to meet a parent? What's your name? How old are you?"

"I'm late for a meeting, can we get someone from HR down here?"

"She looks sort of familiar, you know what I mean?"

"Has she been in EastEnders?"

"You watch EastEnders? You muppet!"

I hear so many voices, but I'm having trouble processing what's being said. When I open my eyes, there's a plethora of concerned faces looking down at me. The first thing I do is smile. A smile gets you a long way and it's one of the few powers I still have.

"She's pretty fit," says a boy, barely older than me.

"Too posh for you, Rakesh, this one's upmarket Chelsea totty," says his friend.

"Where am I?" Sitting up is not as easy as it sounds. I'm lying on a comfortable leather sofa and I never want to leave it. Plus, with so many heads looming over me, I just want to bury myself under the cushions.

The distinguished gentleman from outside helps me to sit forward. I'm in the lobby of One Canada Square. I came here with Daddy about a year ago. There are the usual tables with corporate magazines, a bar, mood lighting, a large reception area and lots and lots of brown marble. In fact, it's very similar to the lobby in G-

Netik's HQ, my father's company, right down to the large security guard hovering anxiously behind my small crowd.

The distinguished gentleman hands me a glass of water and makes everybody else stand back to give me some room.

"You're safe. You were on your way in here, were you coming to meet someone? Your father or mother?"

"My uncle." Even though my head is woozy, I find it easy to make things up. Telling lies is a defence mechanism. When I had my powers, I never really needed to trust anybody. Now I have to be more careful. I smile again. I hope I look demure.

"His name is Edgar Masters," I explain. That bit is true. "He's going to take me to lunch." Back to the lies again. Edgar has no idea I'm coming. "He's a hedge fund manager or something." True.

"Yes," says the distinguished gentleman, clearing his throat. "I'm aware of your uncle."

There's an edge to his voice. I didn't know Edgar was that well known. The distinguished gentleman asks the security guard if he would telephone Mr Masters' office and invite him to come down to the lobby.

I just sit there, waiting, while enquiries are made. People keep asking me if I'm ok. I make up a story that I've just recovered from some kind of bug that I caught whilst helping to build schools in Africa. That's enough to encourage the crowd to disperse, no doubt terrified of catching an unknown tropical disease. Only the distinguished gentleman remains. He asks my name.

"Lilly," I say.

How long have I been unconscious? My face could have been picked up by a dozen or more CCTV cameras, or somebody could have recognized me.

"I hope you're feeling better, Lilly. I'll stay with you until your uncle arrives. Are you on school holiday?"

"Yes," I say. "My uncle said he might be able to give me some work experience."

The distinguished gentleman looks surprised again.

"Really? Well..." He looks like he's choosing his words carefully. "I think that's an excellent idea. I know how competitive the job market is, particularly for young people. Although, aren't the holidays nearly over?"

WHERE'S LOLLY?

"I've still got two weeks left. Since I came back from the charity project in India, I've been helping out at a homeless shelter, but I wanted something commercial to put on my CV."

"That's admirable," enthuses the gentleman, then his brow furrows. "Although I thought you said you'd been to Africa?"

"Africa then India," I recover. That's the problem with lies. When you're so carefree about them, you forget what you've said and to whom.

"My word," says the gentleman. "You're quite something, Lilly. I wish my son was as dynamic as you are. I can't wait to meet your uncle and tell him what a delightful young lady you are."

He wouldn't say that if he knew the truth about my pretend uncle.

"Are you close to your uncle?"

"Not really," I say. Odd question. What's he getting at? "Daddy doesn't even know I'm here. I don't think they get on." The words are coming out faster than my imagination can catch up. "But he's still my uncle and I thought it would be a good idea to get to know him."

"I see," says the gentleman, and he's nibbling at his bottom lip. "Good for you. But perhaps you should inform your father. There might be a good reason why he doesn't want you to see–"

He stops at the sound of echoing footsteps above the general hubbub. I look up. A tall man with slicked-back blonde hair and a pin-striped, three-piece suit is marching towards us. I haven't seen Edgar for over a year but it's definitely him. I'm embarrassed to say it but I shiver slightly. I've had a crush on Edgar Masters ever since he visited us last summer at Wentworth Manor, which is my and Daddy's home in Suffolk. I was his tennis partner.

He's incredibly good looking for an older man. I think he's in his mid or late forties. He's older than Daddy, anyway. But you'd think he was in his early thirties.

Edgar's got an amazing body. I got to see that for myself when he took a dip in our swimming pool. Plus, he has this self-assured, charming smile, and a steely look in his eyes.

Looking back, I'd assumed it was just a stupid schoolgirl thing, but, seeing him now, I still really fancy him.

His usual confidence is shaken when he catches sight of me, though. No doubt he's been watching the news.

There's something else, too. I make him uncomfortable, I know that. Especially when I propositioned him the evening following the tennis match. Edgar ran a mile and avoided me for the rest of the weekend.

"Lauren?" he says, guardedly. He looks again at my companion, trying to work out what is going on.

My gentleman looks equally confused, as he stands up and reaches out a hand to Edgar.

"Lauren?" he queries, looking back at me. "I thought you said your name was Lilly?"

"That's my first name. Lilly is my middle name, but it's the name I always use." You see, the lies come so easily.

"Oh, er, I see," says the gentleman.

Edgar shakes his hand.

"Edgar Masters."

"Geoffrey Poulter."

That's interesting. Geoffrey knew of Edgar, but Edgar clearly has no idea who Geoffrey is.

"Well, thank you, Geoffrey, for entertaining my niece."

Edgar looks wary. He didn't feel comfortable saying the word 'niece'. I'm enjoying his discomfort.

"You're welcome. The poor thing had a funny turn. I thought I'd better sit with her until you arrived. If you don't mind me saying, you seem surprised to see her?"

"Uncle Eddie, you haven't forgotten you're taking me to lunch, have you?"

Edgar adjusts his tie.

"What am I like?" he says, in that charming self-deprecating manner. He's recovered well. "Apologies, Lauren. Why don't we, uh...." he tails off.

It's time to help him. I don't want Geoffrey to mention my fainting fit to Edgar.

"I'd love to see your office first, Uncle Eddie."

"Uh. Yes, of course. Although it won't be very interesting for you."

Edgar is going to need a little extra persuasion, but that shouldn't be difficult.

"It's so hot outside at the moment," I say. "I'd just like somewhere to sit down for a while."

The appeal has worked on Geoffrey, who turns to Edgar and says, "Seems like a sensible idea, my dear chap. Poor thing is quite pale. There's not a problem, is there? Would you like me to come too?"

"No, everything is fine." Edgar feigns confusion. "I'm terribly sorry, bad morning, that's all. Come on Lolly, I mean Lilly, let's get you upstairs."

That causes me to smile. Geoffrey is a little taken aback when I kiss him on the cheek and thank him for being such a gentleman.

"One thing, my dear, and with your uncle's permission?" Geoffrey looks enquiringly at Edgar as he takes a business card out of his pocket.

Edgar just raises a polite eyebrow, as if giving his assent.

"May I just say that I've been very impressed with you. My company runs an intern program and we're always looking for exceptional young people. I know how difficult the job market is these days, and if your uncle is too busy to give you proper work experience, please do call me."

"Thank you very much," I say politely, and put Geoffrey's card in my bag.

Edgar leads me away. We walk in silence past the security barriers and into a lift, which whisks us up to the 38th floor.

Chapter 3

Edgar's office is pretty much just that. It's nothing special. It comprises three different areas.

There's the outer area with a busy-looking desk, but nobody sitting at it.

"My PA, Mary, is at lunch," says Edgar, indicating the empty space.

Edgar's desk is separated from his PA's by a glass wall.

Then there is a third area, double the size of the adjoining two. Again, it is separated by a glass screen. There's a boardroom table in there, so it's obviously a meeting room. There's a TV mounted on the wall, some cupboards and not much else.

All the glass, metal and reflective surfaces give me a headache.

Once the door is shut, Edgar pulls up a chair for me in front of his desk, then sits on his own. It's like he's using the desk as a safety barrier.

"You seem nervous, Uncle Eddie."

He runs his fingers through his hair.

"I must say this is most unexpected, Lauren."

"Lolly. Everyone calls me Lolly. Why don't you call me Lolly?"

Edgar is not in the mood to be playful. He never is around me.

I'm feeling much better in the cool and the quiet of this room. It feels like we're isolated from the rest of London. I look out of the window. The view across the city is amazing. I'm like a princess in a tower.

"What's happening with your father?" he asks.

Just thinking about Daddy makes me profoundly sad.

"How much do you know?"

"Only what I read in the papers. I saw the big story about G-Netik. Human rights protestors tipping blood down the walls of the research facility. Your father stepping down as CEO and going off to live on a Caribbean island. What's going on? I haven't been able to contact him. Is he all right?"

"No, he's not," I say, unable to keep the anger out of my voice. "The Security Service have locked him away somewhere."

Edgar goes pale.

"Do they know about his...?"

Edgar can't say the words.

"His unusual abilities?" I finish. "His power to control people? Yes. They know."

That is Daddy's unique gift. He has the power to make people do anything he asks. Edgar is one of the very few people who know about Daddy's 'superpowers' – and about mine.

"Then he's in big trouble," Edgar concludes, gravely. "And they are after you, too? Of course, now I understand the news stories." He rubs his hands wearily over his face.

"Am I to expect a knock at my door next?" he asks, worriedly.

I hadn't even thought about that.

"I doubt it. I don't think they care about Daddy's money, only his abilities and G-Netik's research. Besides, Daddy would never betray you."

Edgar is staring at me, trying to take it all in.

"You'll forgive me, Lolly, but your father never told me how much you know about our arrangement."

Edgar is being very cagey, as well he should.

"I know that you handle Daddy's special accounts."

Edgar smiles thinly, but says nothing. He still doesn't want to give anything away.

"I know that aside from G-Netik's business accounts and Daddy's regular bank accounts, he also has numerous secret funds all over the world, which you manage for him. Daddy was always careful and he believed in forward planning. He told me that if anything should happen to him, if ever our plans went wrong and he went missing, then I was to come and see you."

I stand up and walk to the window. I need to breathe deeply.

"Yes, of course," Edgar says, slumping in his chair. All of a sudden he's less guarded. "You poor thing. I had no idea."

It's a relief to talk to somebody about it, to be honest. Not to be lonely anymore. I'm not saying I trust Edgar, because I don't trust anybody. But Daddy always said that Edgar loves money and you could rely on him to nurture it like it was his baby. And that's what I need right now: money. I have to start planning how I'm going to rescue my father, and somewhere along the line that is going to involve paying people. The truth is, I just need to be with somebody familiar right now.

"Did you know that I had a crush on you last summer?" I can't resist saying it, just to see his reaction.

He looks up sharply. Eventually he breaks out into a smile and a nervous laugh. He gets up from his desk and crosses to a cabinet in the wall. He pours two glasses of water and hands one to me.

"You always were mischievous, Lolly. And yes, I did rather get that impression last time we met."

He's relaxed all of a sudden.

"I can get you money," he says, settling back into his chair. "I'll create a series of accounts for you. You'll need several, just in case. MI5 will be tracking you. And you'll need some false identities, too."

"You're wonderful," I say, happily, perching on the edge of his desk. He has the same broad-shouldered reassurance that my father has, and such piercing blue eyes that they almost don't look real.

"But it's going to take a few days," he warns. "Where are you living? How are you keeping out of sight?"

"I have my methods," I say, airily. I don't want him to know I've been living in an appalling student house for the last two days. I got friendly with some boys. I chose them carefully. They're too wasted to read the news so have no idea who I am. I told them I was travelling, visiting London from Switzerland. They believed me and invited me to 'crash' at their hovel.

"I know you do," says Edgar, with a wry look. He's seen me in action. "But it might be safer and more prudent if I find you somewhere to stay. I have an apartment in Mayfair that you can use."

"Are you installing me in one of your love nests?" I ask, delightedly. Oh yes, I know all about those. I'm very good at

WHERE'S LOLLY?

eavesdropping. Edgar is married but has a certain reputation, apparently. He looks shocked and tries to cover.

"It's an apartment I use when I'm working late, which I frequently have to. But don't worry, you'll have the place to yourself," he says, hurriedly.

I smile and edge myself closer to his chair. His smile wavers and he starts fidgeting.

"You'll come and make sure I'm all right though, won't you?" I ask teasingly. I reach out to stroke his arm. He stops me, politely but firmly.

"Lauren, your father is trusting me to help you. Please. Just... behave yourself will you?"

Bless him, he's almost pleading.

"Ok," I say.

To be honest, it's just an act. My outward persona is all I have at the moment. Edgar expects to see the confident, powerful, self-assured Lolly Rosewood. And I can do that for a while. But I am so tired.

He stands up and rubs his hands together.

"Let's get going. The sooner you're out of sight, the better," he says, scooping up a set of keys from the desk. "And I know what your appetite is like, so I'll arrange for plenty of food to be delivered."

He's lucky I'm not sick over him.

Chapter 4

Edgar's apartment is more like what I am used to. It's large, light, airy and tastefully decorated, if a bit masculine in its minimalist design. Tiled flooring and lots of creams and whites on the walls. But there is also some rather eye-opening artwork – definitely a man's choice – and a proliferation of TV screens in every room.

The sitting room has a very inviting L-shaped leather sofa, a cosy fire to offset the stark decor, and a long glass table on which I spy a woman's scarf. It could belong to Edgar's wife, I suppose. But there's no other indication that a woman has ever been in this place. No, this is Edgar's bachelor pad. His playboy mansion. Or, as I said originally, his love nest.

"I'll arrange for some clothes to be delivered to you. You can use this bedroom," says Edgar.

At first glance, my bedroom looks very similar to the sitting room. White walls, lots of windows, white furniture and tiled floors. But the bed is massive and I long to just flop onto it and sleep for a year. There's some more tasteless, racy artwork above the bed. A naked woman, naturally.

"Don't tell me – you don't know much about art, but you certainly know what you like?" I joke.

"Er. Yes, quite," says Edgar.

I'm enjoying embarrassing him.

"Don't go out and don't answer the door to anyone," he warns me. "It's possible that MI5 or the police or whoever might already have picked you up on CCTV. Let's just hope they didn't trace you to me. I guess I'll find out if I get back to the office and they've arrested Mary."

He doesn't sound that concerned. I guess having worked with Daddy for so long, Edgar is used to being at risk from the authorities. And my distinguished gentleman gave me the impression that he regarded Edgar as some kind of crook. That's as may be, but Daddy considered him a genius with regard to handling money.

"Treat the place as your own," says Edgar. "I'm sure you will anyway."

He walks to the front door.

All of a sudden I feel very alone again. The last couple of hours has been nice and I don't want it to stop. Ok, so Edgar isn't exactly jumping for joy to see me, but at least he's a friendly face.

"You're going?" That sounded too needy. Not cool, Lolly.

"I have to start making some calls don't I?" He's all brisk and businesslike, just like Daddy.

"Are you coming back later?"

"Yes. But I don't know what time. I'll bring food with me. Watch some TV if you like. Amazing, like being at the cinema. I had a whole new series of screens installed last week."

And with that, he's gone, and I'm left feeling wretched.

Chapter 5

I spend the afternoon asleep. I was shattered. The last thing I
remember was clambering across the king size bed, my head
touching the pillow, and that was it.

I'm woken by a loud bang. Instantly my heart starts thumping,
I sit up sharply and my head swims. For a few seconds I don't
know where I am. Stars swim before my eyes, my mouth tastes
disgusting and my hair is plastered across my face and eyes.

"Did I wake you?" asks a voice.

I pull my hair back and my vision finally steadies. Edgar is
standing in front of me, holding an armful of dresses. Slowly, I
realize that two women are behind him in the hallway. They are
holding bags from various boutiques, which they set down before
silently departing.

I just sit on the bed, struggling to make my mouth work,
looking at Edgar like some kind of rag doll. This is so not me. My
dress is crumpled, my hair is everywhere and I just bet I've got
those lines on my face from the pattern on the pillow.

"Have you done this before?" I manage.

Edgar smiles thinly.

"A friend of mine is a personal shopper. I asked her to arrange
it. She's very good. Have you eaten?"

The mention of food makes me want to heave.

"Later," I say, swallowing back bile.

Edgar just keeps looking at me. What is it? What is he
thinking?

"You seem different from the last time I saw you," he says,
thoughtfully.

"Yes. I'm a sophisticated woman now," I joke. For some reason, I don't want him to know that I don't have my powers. I want to be the same dazzling Lolly that he remembers. I don't want pity.

He smiles politely and heads for the door.

"Edgar, wait." I struggle off the bed and trot after him. Why is he so desperate to leave? He looks around, surprised.

"Is there any news of my money and ID?" Of course there won't be, but maybe the conversation will delay him leaving.

"Lolly, it's only been a few hours," he says, patiently. "But don't worry, it's all in hand, I promise."

I feel myself go all soft when he says those words. I like being taken care of. It's what I'm used to.

"I'm also making some enquiries about your father," he adds.

"You're going to help me find him?" That would be incredible. I didn't think for a second that Edgar would have those kinds of connections. "How?"

"I know some dodgy people," he says, honestly. "Not the kind of people you'd play tennis with at your father's mansion. But they are the kind of people who can get fake IDs at short notice. Plus, I have a few friends in the establishment. Someone, somewhere, will know where your father is being held. Sooner or later, I'll find him."

Music to my ears. If Edgar can track down Daddy by the time I make a full recovery, then I'll be able to rescue him and we'll back at Wentworth Manor within a week.

The bubble bursts when Edgar opens the door and steps into the corridor outside.

"Please stay," I plead. "Just for a while. Don't you want to see me in my new dresses?" It sounds so lame. He looks down on me with what is probably pity.

"I'm sorry, Lolly. Maybe tomorrow. But I have to get home. It's my and Lucille's wedding anniversary. I'm taking her to Roux at the Landau."

"Oh." My voice sounds so small, even to my ears. So I'm on my own.

The door closes and the silence pushes at my insides.

Chapter 6

It's morning time. Ten o'clock. I've been in bed for over 14 hours. I slept in my clothes and I feel utterly gross.

I have a bath and change into blue skinny jeans and a black roll neck. I feel human again for the first time in a week.

There's nothing to do so I sit on my bed and try an experiment to see if my powers are coming back. I have the ability to create fire out of my hands. I'm very good at it. I can hurl flame bolts, throw a stream of fire, and even control a raging inferno. You'd be amazed if you could see it. I have no idea how it's possible. 'It just is,' as Daddy is fond of saying.

I stretch my hands out in front of me, cup them together, palms facing upwards. Something simple first, I'll just try conjuring up a small flame. I concentrate... and concentrate. There should be something. I can feel my stomach tightening until it hurts. I feel weird and I have to stop. I'm out of breath.

I give up and explore the kitchen instead. It's huge. There's a nice view of Hyde Park from here.

The fridge and cupboards are full. Edgar must have come back while I was asleep and stocked up.

Thankfully, the sight of food doesn't make me sick. That's a novelty. I spy a box of biscuits and I take one out. A plain digestive. I'm able to eat it and keep it down. I can't manage anything else though, so I just pour myself a glass of water. Then another. I'm so thirsty, and within a few minutes I have drunk two pints.

I hear a key in the lock. My excitement that it is Edgar returning overwhelms my caution and I dash to the door.

I stop short. I'm looking at a woman, probably in her mid twenties, blonde, pretty and open mouthed with the same look of surprise that I'm probably expressing.

She looks around nervously, like maybe she's just walked into the wrong apartment.

"Who are you?" she asks.

"Lilly," I lie again. I didn't even need to think about it. "Who are you?"

As I ask the question, my brain catches up and I know exactly who she is. Edgar's mistress, of course, the owner of the scarf and current frequenter of the love nest.

"What are you doing here, Lilly?" The woman is guarded. She's instantly on the defensive. I bet all sorts of thoughts are whizzing through her mind. Am I another girlfriend? Has she been replaced?

"I'm Edgar's niece," I say. Best to stick with just one lie. I can't cope with any more at the moment.

She's still cautious. Probably wondering if I'll tell Edgar's wife about her.

"It's ok, it's cool," I assure her. "I know about you and Uncle Eddie. Really, it's cool." The last thing I want is a fight. Instantly, she relaxes. She's delighted, in fact.

"Oh, thank goodness. I mean, I'm sorry about your aunt, his wife. But it's a relief, you know. He said he would tell her about me, but, I guess after all this time I didn't believe him." She looks like a bomb that's just been defused.

Oops. What have I done? I just smile. She obviously doesn't know Edgar like I do. Lies come even more easily to him than they do to me.

She's nervous and that makes her animated.

"I'm Cassie," she reaches out a hand and I shake it politely. "Is Eddie here?"

"No. I think he's in the office. He's got something majorly important to do." Like finding my father and arranging my new life.

"Course he has," says Cassie, laughing. "Stupid me. He's got a lot to sort out. I promised I wouldn't hassle him."

Now *I* don't know what *she's* talking about, but I let it go.

"I simply must have a cup of tea," she says. "I'll make you one."

I follow her into the kitchen. She opens a cupboard and sees the food.

"Wow. Is this all for you?"

"Uncle Eddie got it delivered yesterday, but I'm not very hungry."

"Which means you are, but you're counting the calories, right?" she says, laughing. "Not that you need to. You've got a gorgeous figure, in fact you probably need feeding up. My personal trainer has set out all my meal plans, totally low in fat, but they still fill you up. I can give you the recipes if you like?"

She's very friendly and bubbly and go-getting. I can see why Edgar likes her. There's something else I see in her demeanour, too. Her family are from 'old' money. One can always tell.

She makes us tea and we go through to the sitting room.

"So..." she begins, sipping her tea. "You're Eddie's niece. So you must be Pru's daughter?"

Prunella is Edgar's sister who lives in New Zealand. Edgar hasn't heard from her for years, so it's highly unlikely that Cassie knows anything about her. Therefore I'm safe to pose as her daughter.

"That's right. I've been travelling. I've been in Africa, now I'm in the UK for a while so I thought I'd look up Uncle Eddie."

"Wonderful. I wish I'd done something like that in my gap year, but I spent all the time skiing."

"How long have you been with Uncle Eddie?"

Cassie blushes. She's coy about what she should say.

"Oh, some while. And right from the beginning, he told me about his wife," she says, urgently. "And I told him I wasn't interested, but when I saw how unhappy he was with Lucille and how they were going to split up anyway, well..." She lets the sentence tail off.

I almost feel sorry for her. Almost. 'Some while' is probably something like two or three years. I've seen a lot of girls like this one. Mummy left Daddy when I was very little. Since then, my father has had dozens of girlfriends. They were all besotted with him, all thinking they were the One. Daddy was always very honest with them, always said he'd never marry again. It was for their own good, really. His superpower makes relationships very difficult.

Cassie has that same hungry look in her eyes as they all did. She wants to be Mrs Edgar Masters so badly that it hurts.

"I'm sure you'll be very happy," I say.

There's an awkward silence. Maybe she sees the scepticism in my eyes. She gets up.

"I'm just going to give Eddie a call, let him know I'm here and that I've met his charming niece."

She straightens her skirt, takes her phone out of her deep blue Prada tote, and heads for the hallway.

I hadn't registered it before, but she was clutching some brochures when she came in. She's left them on the glass table. I lean over to look. They are for houses, and by that I mean grand, exclusive properties, like Wentworth Manor.

Edgar obviously has a type: blonde and with a rich heritage. Edgar's wife looks like an older version of Cassie, and her family are exceptionally wealthy. Daddy told me that Edgar made his fortune using Lucille's money. I'm not blonde and I don't have a penny yet, which probably accounts for why Edgar isn't interested in me. But then I've never been one to accept defeat.

Cassie comes back into the sitting room. She smiles, innocently.

"I couldn't reach him. I texted Mary, his PA. She said he had to go to a meeting. I left Eddie a voicemail, though. I told him how thrilled I was that he'd finally told people about me. Not that he ever made me feel like a dirty little secret or anything," she adds, hastily. "But you know."

I nod sagely.

"Mary knows. She's very sweet. We get on pretty well," she adds. "She's my little confidant."

Cassie sits down and neatens the pile of brochures. I can tell that she's dying to show me them, but is probably wondering how prudent that would be, before she's spoken to Edgar. In the end, she says nothing.

Suddenly she looks alarmed.

"It's not what you think, you know."

I'm not sure what she's talking about.

"I'm not after him for the money, honestly."

"I didn't think that." It's so nice to tell the truth occasionally.

"My family is, you know." She cuts off. It would be indiscreet to talk about her family's wealth. She sees that I understand.

We sit drinking our tea in silence.

"I hope you don't mind me saying, sweetie," she says eventually, "but you're looking a bit peaky. Bit off colour. Would you like me to make you some lunch?"

I shake my head and get up. All of a sudden I'm really hot, almost burning up. The roll neck feels like it is choking me. I desperately need a glass of water. I know I won't be sick again because there really is nothing left to bring up. I take one step towards the kitchen and my vision swims. Not again! I feel my legs give way and the side of the glass table is suddenly in front of my face. I hear a horrible crunching sound and then nothing.

Chapter 7

I wake up and I know the routine now. I don't know where I am, my vision jumps like I'm balancing on a jackhammer, my stomach feels like there is a brick in it and my mouth tastes disgusting. This time I have the most shocking headache.

"Oh sweetie, you poor thing, thank goodness. I was about to phone for an ambulance."

It's Cassie's voice. She is kneeling down beside me on the floor, dabbing at my bloody forehead with a wet wipe.

"Take it easy, Lilly. I'll help you get up. You had a nasty fall and you bumped your head. I don't think it's serious, though."

Of course it's not serious. If she knew the kind of people I've been in fights with, how much of a clattering I've taken over the last two years, she'd know that a cut forehead isn't going to bother me.

I touch the source of the pain, just above my left eye. It's sticky and wet, and there is blood on my fingers. It's weird. I can't remember the last time I had an injury that didn't heal within a few minutes. Another benefit of my superpowers.

Cassie is talking, but I can't take in what she's saying. Eventually she leaves the sitting room. I don't know how long it is before she returns, carrying a tray with a bowl on it. It's soup. She's made me soup! Broccoli and stilton by the smell of it, one of my favourites. There is some bread on a separate plate on the tray.

She sits down on the sofa next to me and rests the tray on her lap.

"I made you this. You really should eat something, Lilly. My mother always made me this when I was poorly."

Amazingly, the thought doesn't repel me. I actually feel like I could manage something.

She passes over the tray. My hands are shaking and I'm unable to hold the spoon properly. Gently, Cassie takes the spoon from me, dips it into the bowl and brings it up to my mouth. I feel like a child again. Why is this woman being so nice to me? She doesn't even know me. This is not what I'm used to. I can't understand her at all.

The soup is delicious. I haven't eaten in a week, save for one biscuit, and this tastes like nectar. Instantly I feel the warmth in my tummy, the flow of blood through my veins, my stomach rumbles demanding more, and Cassie gives it to me. I'm not used to feeling helpless. I'm at a loss for words. I don't do gratitude. It's so not me.

I can't manage all of it, and I can't eat any of the bread, but I do feel a lot better.

I get up, somewhat unsteadily, to use the bathroom. While I'm there, I look in the mirror. There's a massive egg-shaped bruise coming up above my eye. At least it has stopped bleeding.

If I could just eat more I'd have my powers back, and that injury would be gone. It's maddening.

When I get back to the sitting room, Cassie has already cleared away the lunch things.

"I've just heard from Eddie, he's coming over," she says, excitedly. "I told him about your accident, but he didn't seem that bothered. What kind of uncle is he?"

I smile weakly. Edgar wouldn't expect me to get injured at all, was the answer to that question. I'm glad that he's coming, though. I want him to take care of me.

***

Edgar arrives just after one o'clock. Despite what Cassie said, he is actually very concerned about me. The look of surprise on his face when he sees the lump on my forehead almost matches his expression when he saw me in the lobby of One Canada Square.

Cassie looks a bit miffed as he gives her a hurried peck on the cheek and walks on past, towards me.

"Lolly, are you all right?" he asks meaningfully, placing his fingers on the bruise as though checking it is real. I try not to flinch because it is the only time he has touched me, but it hurts and he sees that.

"Her name is Lilly, not Lolly, silly," says Cassie. "Oh, that sounds funny, doesn't it?" She is pleased with her joke. "Don't you know your own niece's name?"

"Family joke," says Edgar, dismissively. "What happened?"

"She's obviously sickening for something. Probably picked it up in Africa. She fainted and hit her head. I nearly called an ambulance."

Edgar's eyes widen.

"You didn't, though?" he fires at her.

"No," she says, a little taken aback. Then she brightens up. "Lilly told me that she knew about us. Thank you, Edgar, thank you. I know you said you were going to tell your wife and family, but... well, you know."

Edgar never takes his eyes off me.

"Well, a promise is a promise, baby," he says coolly. "Actually, Cassie, will you give me and Lo— Lilly some space. There's something I need to talk to her about."

"Oh. Yes. I guess." She looks put out again. "But if it's about us, then shouldn't I be here too? You know, if we are all going to be a family?"

"Sure, baby. But this is about Lilly and her, er, illness. Something her father asked me to talk to her about. I'm sure you understand."

Cassie knows she's not going to get her way on this one.

"Yes. Of course." She picks up her bag. "I'll be in our bedroom."

I like the 'our'. In her mind, she and Edgar are already married. She trots along the hallway. Edgar closes the door to the sitting room, then looks back at me.

"Seriously, Lolly, what's going on? You're hurt. How can you be hurt?"

"It's a long story." And not one I'm particularly proud of or want to go into with him. "I'll be fine."

"But you're not fine." He's close to me now; he's not jumpy, just tender. His fingers lightly brush my temple, he smooths a lock of hair away from my eyes, and peers closely at the cut and bruise.

"Really, I am," I insist. "It's a temporary thing. I was injected with a drug. It's kind of upset my body. I'll get over it."

"What about your other powers? Strength? The flame power? All those acrobatic things you do?"

"Still got those," I lie. Don't ask me why. I just hate him seeing me this vulnerable.

"Thank goodness," he says. "You know I'll do everything I can to find your father, but rescuing him will be down to you, and if you're going up against the police you're going to need all your powers."

A rather obvious statement, but at least he cares. Is it my imagination or is he warming to me slightly? Perhaps he actually responds to the vulnerability thing. Maybe all the time I was super strong it was undermining his masculinity or something. I guess he just likes to be the protector. Which is sweet.

"How are things going with that?" I ask.

"Good and bad. My contacts are on the trail of your father. I may have news by the end of the week. Also, bank accounts have been set up and the ink is drying on the IDs now. But there is a problem."

There always is, isn't there.

"Your father is a very cautious man. Wisely, as it turns out. Although I arrange all his private banking, naturally I cannot withdraw funds or move them into your new accounts without his password."

Logical. Daddy may like Edgar, but he only trusts him so far. There's only one person that Daddy trusts implicitly and that is me. Daddy's password is Darl1ng_EmM4. Emma is Mummy's name. My father still loves her, you see. And as much as I like Edgar, I'm not about to give him Daddy's password either.

"I can give you money, to keep you going, as it were," says Edgar. "In fact, I took the liberty of transferring £100,000 from my own account across the ten accounts that I have created for you. It's all I can do at the moment without raising suspicion about where the cash is going. I'm sorry, I hope it's enough."

I know I'm a selfish person and I expected Edgar to help me, but I didn't expect this.

"Thank you," I say, genuinely moved. Again, I don't understand why people want to help me. I wouldn't in their position. Edgar doesn't owe me anything, not really.

"But it's all right," I add. "I know Daddy's password. I can help you transfer his money. You don't have to give me yours. Daddy wouldn't want that."

"You know his password?" asks Edgar, sceptically. "Michael must really trust you."

"He does," I say, proudly.

"Ok, well, obviously don't tell me what it is. I'll come back here tonight and I'll bring a laptop. We can arrange the transfer of funds and then you can authorize it. I won't even have to see you type it in. I'll leave the room," he jokes.

"That sounds like a plan, but I'd kind of like you to stay in the room with me," I say, hoping he will take my meaning.

"Lolly, your father and I have an excellent working arrangement. But if he thought I had intimate knowledge of his daughter or his passwords, he would kill me without a second thought. I don't want that hanging over my head." He's saying the words but, unlike last time, he's not backing away. His eyes are as sure as steel and bluer than sapphire. It's me who is trembling slightly. I brush my body against his. He just smiles. Nothing happens, but there is a definite frisson between us.

Daddy probably would kill Edgar if he and I hooked up, but I want to see if Edgar is man enough to take on the challenge anyway.

There's the sound of clomping in the hallway. Cassie is returning.

Edgar takes a relaxed step backwards and is a respectable distance away by the time the door opens.

"Everything ok?" Cassie asks brightly. She's clearly not confident enough in her relationship yet to be comfortable with closed doors and private conversations. Perhaps she knows Edgar better than she realizes.

I nod my head.

"Yes. Nothing to worry about. Uncle Eddie was just saying that my mother used to have similar fainting spells. It could be genetic."

"Oh bless you, you poor thing," says Cassie, relieved now she's privy to a family secret. "Well, I'm sure your uncle can get you the best doctor. Can't you, Eddie?"

"That's what I was just telling Lauren. Er, Lilly. Lolly. No, Lilly."

I laugh and so does Cassie, although she doesn't know why.

"Anyway," says Edgar, turning to his mistress. "I promised to take you to lunch, and that is what we are going to do."

"Oh, wonderful. I fancy somewhere in Covent Garden," she says, excitedly. "Will you join us, Lilly?" She obviously wants to make the most of the family experience.

"I'm really not feeling up to it," I say, sitting down on the sofa to show how weak I am. "Besides, you've got all your plans to discuss. You don't want me there being gooseberry."

"Sure?" asks Cassie.

"Positive," I insist.

"Well, ok," she says. "Actually, Eddie and I do have some important things to talk about." She turns to Edgar. "I discussed that thing with my mother and it's all ok," she says.

"Excellent," says Edgar, briskly. "You get some rest, Lolly."

"Sure," I say. "Now go on, go, be lovebirds, I'll sit and watch TV."

They head for the door. Cassie has left her brochures on the glass table. I almost remind her, but then I can't be bothered.

"I'll come and see you later, Lilly," Edgar says heartily. "To make sure you're ok."

"I might be in bed," I say, deliberately.

Poor Cassie. It goes straight over her head.

Chapter 8

By the time Edgar returns at eight o'clock that evening, I have had another bath, washed my hair, styled it, doused myself in perfume and even put makeup on. I have picked out a beautiful red, full-length evening dress. I still have enough curves to get away with it being clingy and I'm in love with the cutaway neck.

I check myself endlessly in the mirror. I've decided to wear my hair up. Perfect. I want him to see me as a sophisticated, stylish woman.

I'm in the sitting room when I hear the door go. He's on his own, thank goodness. He walks in, all beautiful smile and immaculate suit.

When I see him holding something behind his back, I think he's brought me flowers, but actually it's just a laptop carrier.

"Bank account details are in the bag," he declares, triumphantly. "And so is the computer. You'll soon have your independence again. And the IDs will be ready tomorrow."

Sweet, but somehow I'm disappointed. Maybe he sees it in my face. He walks up to me. His mouth is just centimetres from mine. I like his aftershave. Sweet, subtle and very masculine.

"Were you expecting something else?" He's almost laughing at me.

I shake my head.

"You look beautiful, Lolly," he murmurs. "But even the makeup can't hide your lies."

My stomach does somersaults. What does he mean?

He smiles again and paces back into the hallway. What is he doing? He stands by the front door and takes hold of the handle.

I'm holding my breath. What is he going to do? Please say he hasn't sold me out. For a moment, I picture a corridor full of Security Service agents just waiting to burst in and drag me off to the dungeon next to my father.

He turns the handle slowly, not taking his eyes off me. The door opens.

I brace myself. Then my heart leaps.

"I mean that I know girls always expect flowers on a dinner date," he says, grandly.

I look. There's a huge bouquet in the corridor outside the apartment. He must have left it there, deliberately. Laughing, he picks it up, carries it inside and places it carefully on the same table that I cracked my head on earlier.

"They're beautiful," I gasp. They smell delightful. It strikes me that I've never been bought flowers before. I mean, Daddy has given me flowers, and I've been presented them by various people as part of Daddy's network of business contacts. But never by anybody special, if you know what I mean. I'm stuttering and I don't know what to do with myself.

He places his strong hands on my bare shoulders.

"And so are you," he says. "I never thought I'd be saying that to you, not in the way I mean it now."

My heart is really pounding and I'm so scared that I might faint again. I haven't eaten anything since the soup, and getting ready for tonight seems to have taken all my energy. If he breathes on me too heavily, I think I'll just fall at his feet.

"Am I beautiful?" I ask. I just want to hear him say it.

"Exquisite," he replies, now even closer to me. He kisses me on the forehead, on the edge of my unsightly bruise. The pressure is enough to make me flinch because it still really hurts, but the rest of my skin tingles. He pushes harder. I don't want him to stop, and I don't want him to know how much it is hurting. Eventually he pulls back and the pain in my head subsides.

I want him to kiss me properly, but he's obviously going to take his time.

He backs off.

"I haven't finished yet," he says. There's a knock at the door. This time he opens it and a man dressed in a short white jacket and black trousers pushes a trolley into the apartment. There are silver platters on the trolley and a bottle of champagne and two glasses. I should be grateful. I like the signal it sends out, but I won't be able to eat that food, let alone touch the champagne.

"Cassie said you needed feeding up," says Edgar. "And I wasn't in the mood to cook, so I thought I'd order it in."

Edgar shows the waiter into the dining room, where the man arranges the various items on the dining room table, removes the platters, pours the champagne and seats first me, then Edgar. Then he leaves, quietly and efficiently.

Edgar lifts his glass.

"To you, Lolly, Lilly, whichever name I'm supposed to remember." He laughs.

I raise my glass, sniff it and know that I can't drink. I put the glass down.

He's ordered duck. Usually this is one of my favourites, but the rich gaminess is simply too much. I manage one mouthful of meat and slightly more of the vegetables. It does help.

Edgar eats heartily, but with impeccable manners.

We talk. He asks me about what Daddy was doing at the point he was grabbed by MI5. I tell him a little. I could tell him about the twins, James and Samantha Blake. They are like me, they have special abilities. It was my father's hope that the Blake family and our family would come together, be stronger as a unit, and be a symbol of what people with abilities can accomplish. It didn't quite work out that way.

But actually I don't tell Edgar any of that. For some reason, I don't want him knowing about James Blake. There's something about James that I like. I want to keep him separate from... well, whatever might or might not happen with Edgar tonight.

In turn, I ask him about his real name. It has popped back into my head that he changed his name to Edgar Masters many years ago. Edgar comes from 'humble beginnings', as they say. Daddy told me that he was an obsessive social climber and thought that his new moniker was more befitting to his desired social status.

I can tell by the look on Edgar's face that he does not want to discuss it.

Instead he asks me about my father's investment in the Channel Islands. Edgar arranged for the purchase of a series of small, unconnected islands from the Jersey or Guernsey government – I can't remember which – on Daddy's behalf. This is one of Daddy's few schemes that I know little about. Edgar is disappointed.

***

Once he's finished eating, Edgar invites me back into the sitting room. He picks up the laptop bag, takes the computer out, sits down and switches the machine on.

I sit down next to him on the sofa, leaning in towards him and I tuck my legs underneath my bottom. He smiles, but doesn't look at me. I like this.

As he's pressing buttons, I plant a kiss on his cheek. His grin gets wider, so I do it again.

"Lolly, I'm trying to concentrate," he says, laughing. Now I'm stroking his leg and his eyes open wider.

"Lolly, please," he begs. "I could end up transferring your father's fortune to the cat's home by mistake."

"I've been told I'm like a cat," I tease him. "Would you look after me?"

He hands me a sheaf of papers from the laptop case.

"These are the details of your accounts. I suggest you look at them and make sure you understand what they are. I've set it up to distribute ten million pounds across the accounts. If things change or you need more money, come back and see me."

I take the papers and leave them beside me on the sofa.

"I love it when you're so serious," I whisper in his ear.

Edgar carries on pressing buttons until, eventually, he turns the laptop screen around and I see a password prompt.

"Type it in and the money will transfer to the bank accounts," he says. He looks away, theatrically.

Instead of typing in the password, I just start stroking his neat blonde hair.

"You're impossible," he complains.

"Aren't I? What are you going to do about me?"

He laughs again.

"Finish the transaction, and we'll discuss it."

I type in my father's password.

"Submit," I say, as I click the button with that instruction on it.

A message pops up on the screen.

'Transaction complete'.

I hand the computer back to him.

"That's it. Deal has been executed. Congratulations, Lolly Rosewood. You're now a multi-millionaire."

That does have a nice ring to it. Not that I ever wanted for anything with Daddy. But I've never had a bank account or carried my own money. It's weird knowing that I'm rich.

He shuts the laptop down and puts it away.

"You know, maybe I would like some champagne now, to celebrate," I say.

Edgar nods in approval and goes back to the dining room, returning moments later with the glasses and bottle.

We toast each other and I take a sip. I make sure I hold his gaze and I tilt my head forward slightly, offering him my mouth to kiss.

"I've got my champagne, now I'd like my celebration," I say.

I'm half expecting him to run a mile, like he did when we were in his office. But I can see in his eyes that I've won. He can't help himself. Despite what he said about me being his friend's daughter, he's not going to turn me down now. I'm his type, I know I am. Stronger than Cassie. Someone more his equal.

I close my eyes and I feel his lips on mine. Gentle at first, then more urgent, and instantly I'm in heaven. He is stroking my bare arms. Then he places one hand on my waist and one on my back. I'm almost squirming at his touch.

"Aren't you scared of what my father will do if he finds out about this?" I say, gasping.

"Not as scared as I am of missing this night with you," he whispers, kissing my neck. "In fact, I don't think even your father could persuade me not to do this, right here, right now."

I giggle. He's making a joke. Daddy's nickname is Mr Persuasion, given to him by the journalists, on account of how he always gets his way.

I'm finding out what Edgar's special ability is.

"He might kill you if he ever finds out," I taunt, testing him.

Edgar just smiles, his hands caressing my shoulders.

"I never can resist a rich girl," he says, as he removes my dress.

Chapter 9

I wake up and once again I don't know where I am. It's morning time. I turn over and see Eddie lying beside me. I sigh deeply and remember everything about last night. It was, well, let's just say it was the best night of my life.

Eddie is facing away from me. I can't take my eyes off his smooth, powerful shoulders and his tousled blonde hair. He's very strong.

I feel very small and vulnerable lying next to him, but I like it.

We talked for hours. He's a really good listener. I've never met anyone I can talk to like that before. Actually I've never felt *the need* to talk to anyone like that before. What's happened to me? Losing my powers has turned me into such a stereotypical girl, but with Eddie, it feels ok.

I told him how I got my abilities and how much food I need to eat in order to maintain them. It's a lot. Using my superpowers burns thousands of calories, so you can imagine how much I need to eat to stop myself starving to death. And of course, at the moment, my calorie intake is virtually zero.

The funny thing is, I actually do feel really hungry now. For the first time in days, I can actually eat.

I get up and pad through to the kitchen. Eddie doesn't stir. I make some cereal, butter four slices of bread, and place a few biscuits on the plate. Then I go through to the sitting room. I smile when I see my discarded clothes.

I eat greedily. It feels so good. Maybe better than last night! Love must have been the magic ingredient to help me overcome my illness.

Once I'm finished, I head for the bathroom and step into the shower. I feel revitalized. In a few days, if I keep eating, I should be back to my normal self. I have some bruises on my body but they, like the egg on my forehead, should start disappearing soon.

I wrap a towel around me and head back into the bedroom. Eddie is awake.

"Good morning," he says, sleepily. "How are you?"

"I'm good. Very good. You've made me better."

"Better?" he asks, sitting up.

"I've just managed to eat my first full meal. I'm starting to feel stronger already."

He reaches out to me, so I stand in front of him.

"That's good news," he says, taking my hands. "I'm glad you've got some strength left."

He grins wickedly and pulls me across the bed, as I squeal with delight.

***

Later, I don't feel so good. Despite my pleading, begging and trying to tempt him, Eddie says he has to go into the office. He says he still has to arrange my IDs. I don't care about IDs, I just want to spend the day with him. I want us to make plans, work out how we're going to rescue Daddy, work out how we're going to *tell* Daddy about us.

But he's adamant he's got to go. And he does. Just like that.

As the door bangs shut, I'm left all alone. I'm tired and I ache. I stand in the hallway and shiver.

I'm still wrapped in my towel. I need another shower but I'm too exhausted to go to the bathroom or to eat.

I go into the sitting room and clamber onto the sofa. I spy one of Cassie's brochures. I'd completely forgotten about her. Lovely girl, but very naive, with her dreams of marrying Eddie.

I flick through the pages. Cassie has made some notes on various houses. Her favourite choices, pros and cons, suggestions for interior design; she's even noted down schools. That's forward planning for you. And she's dated all her notes. She really is super efficient. She's only been looking for a few days and she's already planned out their whole lives.

She made her first note four days ago, on Monday the 15th of August. That's two days after the big announcement about Daddy supposedly retiring to the Caribbean. I don't know why that seems significant to me. It just strikes me as poignant that Cassie started planning her new life at the same time mine was falling apart.

And Eddie has told her he is going to leave his wife, even though he clearly has no intention of doing so. So what's Eddie going to do when Cassie says, 'Right, we're buying this house'? How is he going to lie his way out of that one? And is he going to tell Cassie about me?

I'm on too big a high to worry about it, so I crawl back into bed. There's nothing else for me to do until Eddie calls.

Chapter 10

The front door bangs and once again I'm woken up. This is becoming a habit. I assume it's Eddie so I leap out of bed, naked, to surprise him.

But it's me who gets the surprise. Make that 'shock'.

It's Cassie, and she's standing in the hallway, looking at me like I've fallen from a star. At first she's about to apologize for startling me. Her hand flies to her mouth and she looks embarrassed. Then she realizes that I've just come out of 'her' and Eddie's bedroom. I can tell by the way her eyes work back along the corridor to the open door and the unmade bed. Now she's even redder in the face and her eyes are almost popping out of their sockets.

"What were you doing in my bedroom?" she demands. A small part of her brain has probably already supplied the answer, but she's in denial.

"Don't you know how to respect privacy? And for goodness' sake, can't you put some clothes on?"

"I spent the night with Eddie," I say. This time I have no reason to lie. Better she knows the truth.

"What?" she explodes, shaking her head and letting out a semi-hysterical laugh. "Are you quite right in the head?"

I don't bother to answer. I just stand there, contemplating her politely. She'll need to get this out of her system, so I let her. You may think I'm not a very nice person, but actually I'm just being practical.

She's still doing the hysterical laughter thing.

"I thought you were a nice girl. But now I see you've got problems. Why else would you say such terrible things about your uncle."

Ah yes, of course, I'd forgotten that lie. No wonder she's having such problems processing the situation.

"He's not my uncle. He's a friend. I've known him for years."

"A friend?" she says, disbelievingly. "You need help, that's what you need. I think you should leave. Get dressed, take whatever things you have – not your dignity because you must have lost that a long time ago – and get out. I never want to see you again."

"That's not going to happen. I think you should talk to Eddie."

"You think? Who do you think you are to tell me what I should and shouldn't do with my boyfriend? Some stupid little girl who's clearly deluded."

I don't react. Cassie is breathing heavily now and she goes suddenly quiet. Maybe she's working out what to say next.

She swallows so loudly that the whole building must have heard.

"I suggest you go now," she says, struggling to keep her voice even. "I am going to call Eddie, to let him know what an ungrateful, stupid fool he's let into his house." She's already dialling Eddie's number on her phone. I think it's gone straight to voicemail.

"Eddie, this is Cassie. I really need to talk to you about Lilly. I think you should speak to her. We have something of a situation here. Please call me back."

She ends the call, trying to conceal her frustration.

"I'm going to see him now. If I were you, I'd be gone long before I get back."

And with that, Cassie leaves the apartment, slamming the door hard on her way out. It's amazing it's still on its hinges.

I take a deep breath and wander into the kitchen. I idly snack on more bread and cheese. I feel so much better. My confidence is coming back minute by minute. I'm starting to feel more like the real Lolly Rosewood, rather than some helpless little girl.

The apartment phone rings. It could be Eddie. Perhaps he got the voicemail and wants to speak to me. The phone is in its cradle in the hallway. I pick up.

"Lolly?"

I can't stop myself from grinning and hugging myself.

"Hey, mr loverman," I say, in my most coquettish voice.

"Lolly," his voice is urgent and worried.

"That's my name," I sing.

"Lolly, this is serious. You're in danger."

My bubble bursts. This isn't about Cassie at all.

"What sort of danger?"

"I've just had two agents from the Security Service here in my office." He's almost whispering now. "They saw the CCTV footage of you on Wednesday. They saw you enter Canada Square and they've spoken with that old man you were with in the reception area."

This could be bad. Very bad.

"He told them you were seeing me," says Eddie. "Told them you claimed I was your uncle." He lets out a deep groan and swears. I've never heard Eddie swear. I didn't think he knew any swear words and it sounds very odd coming from him.

"What did you tell them?" I ask, my voice suddenly cold. Has he sold me out? No, he wouldn't do that, would he? I have to be prepared, though. Daddy always said the only people we could trust in this world were each other.

"I told them that you came to see me. I explained that I was an old acquaintance of your father and you'd come asking me for money." He pauses for breath. "I said you'd told me you'd run away from home because you'd had a fight with your father, and so I made up a story about giving you some money and that was the last I saw of you."

I let out a silent exhale of relief. Thank you.

"But I severely doubt they believed me," he continued. "And even if they did, the first thing they are going to do is check out all the houses I own and send round people to search. So you need to get yourself out of the apartment now."

He's right. It won't be safe here.

"Ok," I say, flustered.

"Relax. I've made arrangements for you. Take the bank account documents that I brought you and leave. You just need to collect your IDs and you'll be safe. You can go where you like."

"I want to stay with you, though."

"I want that too. But that's not going to happen right now. Don't worry, though, I'll find a way to contact you once I've located your father."

"You promise?"

"I promise. I've got people working on it already. Don't you worry, you'll know where he's being held within the week, and once you've rescued him... well," he chuckles. "Then it's everyone else who'd better watch out."

"Including you, after last night?" I ask, mischievously.

"Yes, well," says Edgar, defensively. "We'll just have to cross that bridge when we come to it. Now, listen. Leave now. Go to this address and my associate will finalize your IDs. He'll need to get some pictures of you. It's a photographic shop on Clapham Road in Oval, called Your Best Day. Got it?"

"Got it." There's some fancy writing pad next to the phone table. Looks like Cassie would have chosen it. It's the only non-masculine thing in the apartment. I write the address down. "But can't you come? I can't go without seeing you."

There's silence on the end of the phone. Then:

"Sure. I'll get there. I can't let you go without seeing you, either."

"Thank you. I'll see you soon, baby."

I wait for a response, but he's already ended the call.

I head back across to my own bedroom and pull out some clothes. Something unobtrusive and practical this time. Grey leggings, a black T-shirt and a navy hoodie. Eddie has even got me some decent trainers.

I dress calmly. There's no reason to panic. No reason to assume the police or MI5 know I'm here. Eddie must have several properties to check, if indeed they are checking at all. Eddie is probably just being paranoid.

I cross to the window and my heart pounds in my chest. There are two police cars and a police van drawing up outside. I'm rooted to the spot. As I watch, another one arrives. Armed police are getting out of the van and they're fanning out around the building.

This is so random. How do they know I'm here? Cassie? Has Cassie finally worked out who I am and tipped them off?

I run into the sitting room and collect the bank account documents and put them in my bag. I'd left half a packet of biscuits on the glass table earlier, so I pop those into the bag too. Then I rip the notepaper with the shop address off the writing pad and exit the apartment, letting the door slam after me. I pull my hood up and walk calmly down the corridor.

My best bet is to head for the roof. The buildings in this part of London are all close together. I may not have my powers, but I should be strong enough to make it across several rooftops and then down to street level to disappear in the crowd.

I'm heading towards the staircase when the unexpected happens. The lift door opens and Cassie strides into the corridor. She's crying, red-faced and clearly on a mission. She's obviously reached the conclusion that I'm telling the truth, or she's come back because she's thought of all the things she wants to say to me. She's halfway down the corridor before she realizes it's me approaching her. Her eyes do that wide-open thing again.

"Oh no," she shouts at the top of her voice, bearing down on me like a tank. "No, no. I decided no. You don't get to just walk away. Not after what you've done!"

I was right. She's lost it.

"I can't believe I tried to help a little slut like you," she yells, belting me across the face with all her might.

It hurts, and she nearly floors me, but if there's a positive to be gained from this experience, it's that the pain rapidly diminishes. There's no burning sensation on my cheek. My abilities are coming back – the healing powers are working!

She hits me again. On the third time I catch her hand, but she's just yelling at me now, calling me all the names that you'd expect. People are opening the doors to their apartments to watch the spectacle. I try to get past her but she's holding on to me like a limpet.

I can't do this now. I have to get out of here before the police make it up to this floor.

Ten metres up ahead, the door to the stairwell crashes open and a policeman in full body armour and carrying a machine gun bursts into the corridor, swivelling first left then right. He sees us.

A colleague is right behind him.

Cassie's so lost in her tirade of invectives that she hasn't even noticed.

"Get off me, you crazy woman," I shout hysterically, as the police approach, guns lowered. I've still got my hood up and they haven't seen my face yet. Two, three more steps and they'll get a good look at me for sure.

I try to back off, but Cassie's hands are clamped to my arms. I scream in frustration.

Then Cassie is dragged off me. It's the first policeman. He's pulled her away and she's struggling. Now he's seen me. He's seen me. I'm paralyzed. I don't know what to do.

"Ladies," the man shouts. "You need to get yourselves out of here. Follow my colleague. Get out, now."

"What are you talking about?" shouts Cassie. "It's her. She's the one you should be arresting. Arrest that slut!"

The second police officer takes my arm now. I'm about to summon every ounce of strength I have left to throw him off, but an instinct kicks in. Something isn't quite right. The man's grip is firm but not rough. He's not trying to subdue me. It's not an attack.

"Please, miss," he says, politely but authoritatively. "You need to follow me out." Then he turns to the people looking out of their apartments. "Everybody else. Just stay inside. Keep the doors shut. Do not open them until you get the all-clear – do you understand?"

The doors close without hesitation.

Officer number two leads me and Cassie back along the corridor, followed by officer one. When we get to the stairwell, officer two leads us down the steps, while his colleague heads on up to the next floor.

What is happening? Were they not given a good description of me? Perhaps the incident with Cassie has confused them. They're expecting the extremely dangerous Lolly Rosewood, not some kid who's having a cat fight with a demented, jilted lover.

I almost can't believe my luck as we're hurried down the steps, with Cassie still shouting. When we get to the ground floor, I hold my breath.

The officer leads us to the main doors. This is the moment of truth. Maybe this is just a trap. They know how dangerous I am. They want me out of the building and in the open where they can take me, en masse? I brace myself. The officer pushes open the door and I'm out into the sunlight.

There's a whole army of police officers waiting for me outside.

Chapter 11

"Keep moving, keep moving please."

A woman with a megaphone is ordering people on the street to get clear of the building. Another officer is gesturing me and Cassie towards portable metal barriers, hastily arranged in a cordon, behind which a large crowd made up of curious members of the general public has already assembled.

Still nobody has tried to arrest me. As soon as Cassie and I are behind the barrier, the officer loses interest. I look back at the apartment and see other people being led out, too.

I giggle as I think of the armed teams inside the apartments, kicking down doors as they search for me, while one of their number has already ushered me to safety. Still, I don't want to push my luck, so I'll get clear of this area right now. I keep my hood up, just to be on the safe side.

Everyone around me is speculating on what's happening inside.

"I heard they got a tip-off about a terrorist," says one man.

"Someone with a bomb or a gun or something," says a woman.

I keep walking. I want to lose Cassie, get to Oval, get my IDs and disappear. As I push my way out of the crowd I try to put the notepaper into my bag, but someone grabs my arm. I turn around in alarm. It's only Cassie. Annoying, but she's the least of my worries.

"Not so fast, you," she says, tugging at me. I pull my arm away. I don't have time for this.

"I'm busy," I tell her.

"Going to meet Edgar? Don't bother, he won't want to see you. I've just spoken to Mary and he's not there."

Of course he's not, you stupid cow – he's coming to meet me.

I say: "Cassie, just drop it. You'll never have to see me again, ok? I'm going. You've got Eddie all to yourself."

What will it take to get this woman off my grill?

"Don't you dare say that, like he's yours to give," she shouted.

Oh no, we're drawing our own crowd. People have grown impatient waiting for the supposed terrorist to be brought out in chains. They want the more immediate pleasure of a girl-fight. This can't be happening.

Cassie is mental. Suddenly she spies the piece of paper in my hand and snatches it from me.

"What's this?"

She looks at the address. It won't mean anything to her, but she can see it was written on the notepaper from the apartment.

"Is this where you're meeting him?" She has the look of a great detective who's just caught the master criminal. "You were sloping off to try and have sex with him again?"

Oh dear. What an imagination. Like I'd go to Oval just to have sex.

"You thought you'd just lose me in the crowd and go and steal my boyfriend?" She's getting hysterical again. One girl in the crowd gets her phone out of her bag.

"Cassie. Listen." I try and keep my tone calm and reasonable. "I slept with him. Get over it. Now I have to leave. You were nice to me, so I'm going to repay the favour. Get real, ok? I probably know more about Eddie than you, and he won't leave his wife, ever. Not for anyone. He's a liar. That's what he does. You've got nothing to offer him. His wife's family is rich and he's always used her to bankroll his deals. Ok? Got it? You're just his bit on the side."

Cassie cackles. Lots of phones have come out now. They're pointing in our direction. We're being filmed. Oh great. Brilliant. MI5 don't have to spy on anyone to find me now, they just have to watch YouTube.

"For your information, miss the-world-revolves-around-me, Eddie is leaving his wife," says Cassie, triumphantly. "And I know all about his money troubles. He told me at the weekend. And I told him that I would give him whatever he needs. So he doesn't need her. He loves me."

I groan. I'm about to point out that if Eddie is taking Cassie's money too, then Cassie is even more stupid than I thought.

But then something clicks in my head. Something that is really not quite right about all of this. I want to vocalize what I'm thinking but, before I can, Cassie slaps me across the face again, and at this the crowd roars with delight. One million hits online, guaranteed, I'm telling you.

"That's for sleeping with him." Cassie almost spits the words at me. "Now, if you know what's good for you, you'll take your stupid, cheap charms, and go and find some other mug to take pity on you."

This elicits a 'wooooh-ooooh' from the crowd. I swear there's not one person left who even cares about the ongoing siege in the apartments.

Cassie stomps off in tears, still clutching the piece of paper. She's going to Oval and she'll see Eddie there and it will ruin everything.

"I'll sleep with you if you want," offers one chav, pointing his phone at me.

I need to think. I'm struggling to concentrate. Something nasty is stirring in my stomach and this time it's nothing to do with my illness. The crowd close in on me. Why am I reminded of witch trials, all of a sudden? Or perhaps I should have a scarlet letter on my forehead? I'm their property now. They want to see some kind of resolution to this. They want justice.

And it's just started to rain. This is incredible. It's like I'm being punished for all my wicked deeds. If you believe in that sort of thing. Which I don't. Which is just as well because I've committed a considerable number and we could be here all week.

I have to make a call. I turn to the young guy who made that most generous of offers. He's still filming me. I want to take the phone with his severed hand still attached to it. I've done a lot worse in my time, believe me.

"I need to borrow your phone," I say. He's dumbstruck. He's from the bottom of the evolutionary pool. I can't believe what I say next.

"I won't sleep with you, but I will kiss you if you let me use your phone and you give me money for the tube."

He's delighted. He hands over the phone and a five pound note. No arguments. He must really be desperate.

I delve into my bag and dig out the phone number for the distinguished gentleman. There it is. Geoffrey Poulter. I ring his number and, thank goodness, he answers.

"It's Lilly," I say. "We met in the lobby of One Canada Square the other day."

"Oh, yes," he sounds surprised but genuinely delighted. "I hadn't expected to hear from you so soon, my dear. How are things?"

"Not so good, really," I say. "I'm in a really bad situation and I need some advice. It's to do with my uncle."

"Ah. Yes. I was afraid of that. I wanted to say something to you the other day. Your uncle has a reputation, but for all the wrong reasons, I'm sorry to say."

I need to get the information that I'm after quickly. Obviously I know that Edgar is crooked. That's why Daddy uses him. But I'm after something specific.

"He wants me to give him money," I say. "I have a very generous allowance, you see. He says it's for a deal that will bring the whole family back together. It'll mend the rift between him and Daddy. But he says I'm not allowed to tell Daddy because it's a secret. I don't know what to do. Do you know why he needs the money?"

Geoffrey clears his throat.

"Well, I would have to say you must talk to your father about this. But I would urge you, and him, not to give Edgar Masters a penny."

"Why not?"

"I'm not one for spreading rumours, but it's the talk of Canary Wharf at the moment. Aside from his long-standing reputation, Edgar has been desperately trying to raise money since the beginning of the week. He's been having meetings like they're going out of fashion. The suggestion is that one of his crooked deals turned sour and he's chasing his losses. That's why I was surprised when you said he was giving you work experience. Not a good environment to be in at the moment. Now my dear, are you all right?"

"I'm fine. I... Did someone from MI5 talk to you at all?" I ask, feeling foolish.

"I beg your pardon?" says Geoffrey, sounding puzzled.

I need time to think.

"Nothing... Sorry. I'll call you back."

I end the call, give the phone back to the chav, kiss him – it's disgusting – and then head off in the direction of Green Park underground station.

I know London pretty well. I've done a lot of work for Daddy, been to a lot of places, so I can get around the city very easily. Often I will run. I can sprint ten times faster and for longer than any Olympic athlete. Except not today.

***

I get to the tube station, but I'm breathing heavily and soaked to the skin by the time I arrive. The rain is heavy. I'm like a drowned rat.

I buy a ticket to Stockwell and get on the Victoria line. I check the map. Four stops. Not far.

It's steamy and oppressive in the tube train. Lots of damp coats, wet hair and hot bodies huddled together.

Some middle-aged man offers me his seat. Incredible. Do I look that bad?

I sit down, close my eyes, pull the hoodie as tight as I can around my face, and think.

And what I'm thinking is that Edgar has sold me out. I don't exactly know why or how, it's just a feeling. And a horrible one, given what we did last night.

First, there is the question of money. I know Edgar is greedy. Daddy said that was good for us, because it meant that he had Edgar's full attention. Daddy needed somebody who was a genius with money to hide it for him. Edgar was that man.

And then there's this sudden urge to leave his wife for Cassie, just days after Daddy gets kidnapped by MI5.

Now I learn that Edgar has had a big deal fall through and he's desperately trying to raise money. Cassie just told me she is going to give him some. And what was it she said to him yesterday? 'I spoke to my mother and she agreed it.' Agreed what? Handing over a large portion of cash – for a big, expensive house, maybe? Or at least that's where Cassie thinks the money is going.

It's not a smoking gun. There's no proof that Edgar has done anything bad to me. Far from it. He's helped me.

What am I missing here? Why are my instincts telling me not to trust him?

Is it to do with last night? When I very first showed up at Canary Wharf, he didn't want me anywhere near him. It felt like he wanted rid of me as soon as possible. That all changed yesterday, once he discovered I had lost my powers. He became softer, attentive. And he couldn't wait to help me. I thought I was seducing him. I thought I'd won my man. I cringe. It wasn't that at all, was it?

I think I've done something very stupid.

He gave me that laptop when I wasn't thinking about anything except the night ahead. Me in my beautiful dress, offering myself to him, thinking I was beguiling him.

I typed in Daddy's password. I can barely think of it. What have I done? I've been so very naive.

I could be wrong. I so hope I am.

This morning he was triumphant, in high spirits, but cold. And now I think back, that's how he was the whole time we were together. It was a cold passion, as though I wasn't really part of what he was feeling, just purely the focus of it. I shiver again.

I look inside the bag. The bank documents look genuine enough, but what will happen if I try and use them? And what's going to happen when I meet this guy in Oval?

I also spy the packet of biscuits that I stuffed into the bag. I start munching on them.

Now I'm thinking of Cassie again. She'll be heading there now to confront Edgar. I presume she's driving. I may get there ahead of her if the traffic is bad. I've never been afflicted by a conscience but, for her sake, I hope I get there first.

I wish Daddy were here to sort this out. But he isn't. So it's down to me. For the first time in my life, I have to sort out my own mess.

Chapter 12

I get off the train at Stockwell and walk along Clapham Road, looking for the photographic studio. It's a long walk and for ages I'm just going past houses and flats.

Eventually I reach a row of shops. With the little change that I have left from my tube ticket, I buy a small packet of sweets in a newsagent. It's still raining and I'm wet through to my bones. I need sugar, so I stuff several sweets into my mouth at once, much to the astonishment of an elderly man in a smart blue blazer.

Clapham Road is endless. I don't know where this photographic shop is, but I see a silver Mercedes convertible pull up a couple of hundred metres ahead of me. Cassie gets out of it. She looks a bit unsteady on her feet. Anger, pain and humiliation must be rattling her nervous system. She's not thinking straight.

I start to run. This time it doesn't hurt so much; the sugar must be doing the trick. I'm sprinting, but at nothing like the pace that I'm capable of. Cassie has disappeared into a shop, so now I know exactly where the studio is. Long before I've got close to it, I've decided I'm not going to use the front door. I prefer rooftops. Strategically it's so much safer to attack from high ground, and my instincts are telling me to prepare for trouble.

Three doors short of the studio there's a narrow alleyway between two buildings. Perfect. I just hope I can do it.

I run straight at the brick wall and jump. I use the momentum to bounce off the surface and upwards, just getting a fingerhold in the uneven brickwork on the opposite side. That's enough to balance me as I drive my left foot against the same wall, and push up again to drive myself higher and back towards the first wall. I repeat the same manoeuvre and that gets me as high as a window ledge. From there, it's simple to pull myself up to the flat roof.

That's better. I feel good.

It's still raining hard, so I have to watch my footing as I run across the slippery tiles. When I'm level with the Mercedes on the road, I know I've reached the right shop.

There's no skylight on the roof, but the shop extends out the front of a much larger building, and where the flat roof begins there is a window set into the wall. I look inside. The glass is so grimy as to be impenetrable, but I don't think there's anybody inside. I try opening the sash window, but it won't move. My muscles strain and finally I break the lock and climb inside.

I'm in a bedroom. A man's bedroom, without a doubt. A man who is not too fussed about hygiene or appearance. It's functional, the bed is unmade, there are numerous pint glasses on the floor, an overflowing ashtray, and piles of clothes. The smell is intolerable. I leave the room in a hurry, but then duck back in because somebody is clomping up the stairs. He's a big man, balding but with a black ponytail and a greying beard. He's wearing dark blue jeans with a Texan-style belt and buckle, a checked shirt, a battered brown leather jacket and cowboy boots. He's carrying two large metal jerry cans. He hasn't seen me and he walks straight into the room that faces the top of the stairs.

It's the bathroom. I hear him unscrewing the lid of a jerry can and emptying the contents into the bath.

I sneak downstairs, careful not to make any noise. Not easy when you're dripping wet and your shoes are squeaking. Fortunately, the guy is making too much noise in the bathroom to hear me.

In the ground-floor hallway there are three doors. One is ajar, so I look through that one first.

Inside I can see a big room, full of photographic equipment. Lights, those umbrella type things, computers, tripods, cameras, green screens, white screens, stools, chairs – all the things you'd expect, and one thing that you wouldn't. Cassie is sprawled out on the floor in front of a plain grey backdrop. I can't tell if she's alive or not. Usually this wouldn't bother me, but I feel a strange sensation in my stomach.

I notice two more of those jerry cans next to Cassie's body.

I don't know what impression you've gained of me by now. Maybe you thought I was a nice girl at first. Sweet and innocent? The girl next door? Believe me, if I lived next door to you, you'd move. I know a lot of what you'd consider to be 'bad people'. Maybe you're getting that now. I know the kind of man the cowboy is, and I know why those containers are there.

He's a killer. And the cans contain acid to dispose of the body. That's why he is upstairs filling the bath. Hired killers are neat. It's not easy to get rid of a body in central London if you don't want any repercussions. The cowboy was obviously waiting for me and he thinks he's done his job. Cassie turned up asking for Edgar and whack, she's down. Edgar doesn't want any comeback from my body turning up in the bins outside some kebab shop. No, he wants Lolly Rosewood to disappear.

But someone else is missing.

The cowboy is a professional killer, but he doesn't own or run the shop. I think Edgar did genuinely arrange IDs for me, before he decided I should die. So somewhere in this building there is a second person – the photographic expert.

I check again. There's only Cassie in this room.

So where's the owner?

I try another door. I'm lucky, because it's the front of the shop. I'm behind the till. The walls are covered by large canvasses and small frames containing photos of perfect men, women and children, against white backgrounds or black and white beaches.

There's a man locking the main door and turning the 'Open' sign to 'Closed'. He's average height, completely bald, more technical than physical and he's nervous.

I'm in my element now. I've done this before.

I place my bag on the floor and march straight up to him, silently and purposefully. He doesn't even see me until it's too late. I grab him by the neck and pin one arm behind his back.

"Sssh, or I'll snap you in half," I whisper in his ear. He can feel the pressure of my hand on his neck and he whimpers. I'll take that as compliance.

"I'm going to ask you some questions," I say. "You're going to answer them. If I think you're telling me the truth, I'm going to let you open the door and leave. If I think you're lying, or holding anything back, you'll be thrown through the door. Do we have a deal?"

I increase the pressure on his neck until he makes a gurgling sound. Then I slacken off.

"Yes," he manages.

"Good boy. Edgar Masters paid you to create IDs, didn't he? Using false names?"

"Yes." No hesitation. He's too scared to fight me.

"Who's the other guy, the cowboy?"

"I... I don't know him. Edgar sent him. Said there'd been a change of plan. He's going to kill the girl, dispose of her. I... I don't want any part of it, but I... I..."

"You do as you're told when there's a trained killer in your shop?"

"Yes."

I don't blame him.

"Are the IDs complete?" I ask.

"Yes. Apart from the photos. They're for some bank accounts."

I consider something he's just said.

"Is the girl dead?"

"No. The guy just hit her. Think he's waiting for confirmation from Edgar before he... y'know."

"What's her name?"

"No idea. Edgar said she'd show up asking for him. Young and pretty, was all he said."

That's something, I suppose.

"Is the cowboy armed?"

"He's got a gun."

Of course he does. He thinks he's a cowboy.

"What's your name?"

"Martin."

"Martin, I'm not going to let you go. I'm not going to kill you, either. I want those IDs. So I need you to do me a favour, will you do that?"

"Y-yes," he says, uncertainly.

"Martin, I'm going to have to trust you, but first I'm going to show you a trick. You see, you've never met a girl like me before."

I release my grip on his neck and hold out my hand just in front of his face. He's breathing hoarsely, but there's no resistance from the arm that I have pinioned.

I just hope my body has recovered enough to give me my flame power back, at least to some degree. My hands are still wet from the rain outside, so it could be tough.

I concentrate, try to conjure the fire in my hands. It hurts. I can feel a strain in my stomach. Then, success. It's not much, but there it is. A perfect flame, like you'd see flickering on a large candle, cradled in my palm.

Chapter 13

Martin gasps, yanks his head back and jerks his body. He's scared. He thinks I'm a devil.

"Martin, if I wanted to, I could burn you alive. You could run, you could try hiding, but it doesn't matter. At any range, I could conjure up these flames and consume your body."

That's not entirely true, but, as you know now, I'm very convincing.

"But I don't want to do that. I want us both to win out here. I'm going to kill the cowboy, you're going to give me the IDs, you'll still get paid and you'll get the other guy's share of the money. Then I'll deal with Edgar, so no comeback on you. How does that sound?"

"S... s... sounds fair," he admits.

"Well, I'm a very fair-minded young woman," I say, all friendly, releasing my grip on him. I even smarten his shirt. "There you go, not even creased, and red is definitely your colour."

"What do you want me to do?" he asks, nervously.

"I want you to pretend you've caught me. You've realized that I'm the girl you were supposed to kill. You'll take me up the stairs to the bathroom so that I can get close to the cowboy, and then..." I let it hang in the air. "Do you know the joke about ponytails?" I ask. Then I remember that my hair is in a ponytail too, so I let it drop. I don't think Martin is in the mood for humour anyway.

I turn around and put my arm behind my back. I look over my shoulder at him.

"Well, take it then," I order. "You've caught me. Force me upstairs – don't worry, I don't mind a bit of rough play."

Timidly, he takes my arm. I groan inwardly. He hasn't got the strength to bruise an apple.

"Put a bit more effort in, Martin," I enthuse. "Be as convincing as you like, this is the closest you'll ever get to a girl as hot as me. But just remember, if you warn the cowboy, then you're toast."

"I won't," he assures me, and pulls tighter on my arm. "Is that all right?" he asks.

Martin really isn't cut out for this sort of work. I'm actually doing him a favour by sparing him the act of killing me and Cassie.

I start walking. Past the till, back into the corridor and to the bottom of the stairs. In fact, I'm leading Martin – he's stumbling as he tries to keep up.

The cowboy is traipsing down the stairs, and when he sees me he whips a gun out from inside his jacket.

He relaxes slightly when he realizes Martin is holding me. I try to look scared and pathetic.

"Who the hell is this?" asks the cowboy. He's got a thick Glaswegian accent.

"I think it's the one we're supposed to kill," says Martin, playing his part. "She said Edgar told her to meet him here."

"Then who's the blonde?" asks the cowboy, irritably, as though the whole thing is Martin's fault.

"Please let me go, I just came here to see Edgar," I beg, trying not to overdo it, although I do love a bit of drama. In fact, this is one of my favourite situations. Big, strong men, preferably trained killers, treating me like I'm a weak and feeble girl. I just love the final looks on their faces when they realize what they are up against.

"Shut your mouth, princess," says the cowboy, marching down the stairs and striking me across the face. I go limp and pretend I'm unconscious.

"Now I come to think of it," says Martin, "I think Edgar did say she was a brunette and younger."

"As opposed to blonde and older?" asks the cowboy, incredulously. "Why the hell didn't you say before? I should kill you, too, for wasting my time."

He's breathing deeply while he's working out what to do. A thick lump like him, it must take a lot of energy to think.

"Ok. Let's take her upstairs. I'll check with the boss and he can call it."

Perfect.

My eyes are closed but I can feel my feet being lifted off the floor, while Martin puts his hands under my arms, and between them they carry me up the stairs. That means the cowboy has holstered his gun. When we get to the top of the stairs, my feet are returned to the floor. And that's the moment.

I open my eyes. The cowboy is facing towards the bathroom door. I punch him in the back of the head. I give it everything I've got and I can feel my knuckles crack. It hurts like hell, but I've given him enough to send him toppling forward so his head makes contact with the sink. Tough guy like that, he'll need more to keep him down so I simply stamp on his head.

Done. He'll be unconscious for a while.

Martin looks at me, terrified.

"What are you going to do?" he asks.

I'd like to dump the cowboy in the acid bath that he intended for me, then kill Martin, too. But I still need those IDs and I don't want to scare Martin unnecessarily.

"We made a deal. I'm prepared to keep it," I say. But I don't want the cowboy to wake up and start again, so I send Martin downstairs, and then I quickly break the killer's neck. My right hand is agony.

The cowboy has a phone in his pocket, which I take. I remove his gun from the holster and drop it into the bath. It plops into the yellowy, evil-looking liquid.

I follow Martin downstairs, looking at my knuckles. They're red and swollen, but if there was any bone damage, it's already healed.

I'm hungry again.

Cassie is alive. She's got a nasty bruise on her right cheek and she's scared, but she's actually pleased to see a friendly face. I help her sit up while she recovers her senses.

"What happened? Where's Edgar?" she asks me. She sees Martin and shrinks into the grey backdrop.

"It's all right," I assure her. "He won't hurt us."

"There's another man," she screeches, pawing at my arm. "He just came at me."

"I know, I know. He's gone. No longer a threat, I promise." I pause a moment and lean in to her. "Cassie, Edgar was behind this."

She looks at me as though she hasn't understood my words at all.

"Edgar set this up to kill me," I say, slowly. "He didn't expect you to come here. You were an accident."

"No, no, you're lying," she says, feebly.

I look back at Martin. He's hovering, uselessly.

"Tell her," I order him.

"It's true," he admits. "But I didn't want to, I swear. Edgar told me to arrange the fake IDs. That's what I do. I do loads of stuff for him. It's how he launders money."

"Edgar isn't a money launderer, or a murderer," insists Cassie, getting to her feet, looking a bit more indignant.

"He's all of that and more," says Martin.

Cassie looks at me, dumbfounded. I check the cowboy's phone. There's a text message trail.

'Potential job for you. Girl. Major problem. Need her to disappear. Will confirm tomorrow. E.' That's the incoming message. No name stored against the number, and it's probably just a pay-as-you-go phone. Edgar wouldn't be so stupid as to use his main phone. But 'E' identifies him to the cowboy, and so it's obvious he has used the ponytailed killer before.

That first text was sent yesterday evening, not long before Edgar arrived at the apartment with the flowers and the laptop.

Below the first text was a second from the same number.

'It's on. Will send her to the studio. Deal with her there. No trace. Will give Martin details of target. Confirm when deal has been executed.' That's a very Edgar-style phrase.

The text is time-stamped at 02:22 this morning. Oh my... He would have been lying next to me in bed. And I thought I was cold.

I show the phone to Cassie. She starts crying. It seems to have convinced her.

I type in a reply.

'Job complete. Should have warned me she fights back.'

I click send.

Within a minute I get the reply.

'Glad you enjoyed yourself. Should have got Martin to film it.'

I take a deep breath. It's time to pay Edgar a visit.

While Cassie finds a chair to slump into, I make Martin finish the IDs. He takes lots of photos and adds them to the driving licenses and passports that are already prepared. He's very good, very quick.

Cassie is in shock.

"He was going to take your money," I explain. "That's how he got started, you know, with his wife's fortune. Some kind of deal must have gone wrong and he was in trouble. He's been trying to cover his losses; it's the talk of Canary Wharf apparently. That's why he finally promised he'd leave his wife for you. You were going to hand over money for the new house to him, weren't you?"

Cassie ignores me.

"I'm going," I tell Cassie, but only Martin seems interested. "If I were you, I'd call the police or get out of here. Actually, I don't much care what you do."

I don't. Martin can keep his money and, if he knows what's good for him, make himself disappear.

"Cassie, I need to borrow your car." She's still not saying anything. "Take care of yourself," I add, a little awkwardly.

I find her bag on the floor and I remove her car keys. On impulse I take her phone too.

"Make her a cup of tea," I say to Martin. She won't come to any harm, not from him. It's weird. I actually kind of like Cassie.

I scoop up my IDs, collect my bag of bank account documents and leave the shop. I get in Cassie's car and drive away.

Chapter 14

Getting back into Canary Wharf is very easy. I simply ask for Geoffrey Poulter, my distinguished gentleman, who tells the receptionist to arrange a pass for me and send me up.

I collect the pass, but I don't go to see Geoffrey. I'm heading for Edgar's office.

I stopped at the apartment on my way here, to confirm some suspicions. I asked around. Apparently the police had been called to the building because somebody had claimed there was a gunman on the roof. Unsurprisingly, it was a hoax.

I think Edgar made that call. He wanted me to see the police turn up in force at the apartment so that it would confirm his story about MI5 closing in on me. No agent came to see him at his office. Edgar's lies are as good as mine. I knew that, but I was blinded by... well, I was very naive.

I helped myself to some more food while I was at the apartment. Some cold chicken, potatoes, cheese, bread and two bananas. My knuckles have healed and I feel great. I even took the time to shower and change out of my soggy leggings. I want to look my best when I see Edgar, so I'm wearing a tailored grey trouser suit with a cream silk top and heels. I check my reflection in the lift as I head up to floor 38. Yes, I look the part.

There are only two things I need now. I need to make sure Edgar hasn't stolen all of Daddy's money, and I need to find out why he has done this. Although greed would seem to be the most likely explanation.

***

I'm sharing the lift with a man and a woman. They eye me with interest because I have a phone in each hand.

Using Cassie's phone, I've already texted Edgar's PA, asking if he's back in the office. He is. I tell her not to let Edgar know I've texted. 'I'm planning a surprise.' How handy that Mary is Cassie's little confidant.

The other phone belongs to the cowboy. Edgar has sent three texts to it, which I haven't answered, all the same: 'Is body disposed?'

It's time to put some dynamite under Edgar's comfy office chair. I send him a reply:

'Two targets arrived. First blonde, then a brunette. Have disposed of both targets.'

The lift comes to a halt at my floor and I exit. I walk slowly down the long corridor. People in suits hurry past me, barely registering my presence.

The cowboy's phone gets another text.

'Should be ONE target. 16 yrs old brunette. Not blonde. Confirm.'

I send:

'Negative. Killed blonde too. Arrived first, asking 4 u, as expected. Driving license says Cassie Beauchamp.'

Suddenly Cassie's phone starts ringing. I let it go to voicemail.

Straight after, the cowboy's phone starts ringing. This time I accept the call and I set the phone to record the conversation.

"What the hell have you done?" It's Edgar. "Tell me you didn't kill Cassie. Tell me you got the brunette."

He sounds desperate.

"Hi, baby," I say. I'm standing outside the door of his office now.

There's silence at the end of the phone. He needs time to think. I'm not going to give it to him.

The door can only be opened with a security card. Or a powerful kick. It swings in with a crash, teetering on its hinges before finally collapsing onto the floor amid the scattering of glass shards.

Mary is at her desk. Surprise – she's young, blonde and pretty. She screams and jumps back, stunned.

I stride in.

"Would you mind staying for a while, Mary," I say. "I may need you."

She doesn't move, so I walk around her desk, take her hand and lead her through into Edgar's office.

I've probably got about ten minutes before someone in another office reports the noise of the door, calls security, and some thick lunk tries to arrest me. Or, if I'm very lucky, everyone will mind their own business because they've got more important things to do than get mixed up with Edgar Masters.

I enter Edgar's office. He's on his feet and he's scared. He's still got a phone in his hand. The pay-as-you-go, no doubt.

He knows I've got my powers back and he doesn't know what I will do with them.

"I hope for your sake you haven't stolen Daddy's money," I say.

"Lolly," he says. "Sweetheart, I was worried about you."

In the last 48 hours I've realized that I never knew Edgar at all. I've seen him tell some convincing lies, but now his talent seems to have deserted him.

I give Mary a little shove to send her around the right side of his desk, then I plant my bottom on the left side, swing my legs over and drive my heels against Edgar's chest. The impact knocks him back into his chair, which bumps against the floor-to-ceiling window. I leave my feet where they are.

I pick up his laptop from the desk and hand it to him. In return, I take the phone he was holding. I look at the screen. The connection is still active.

I check the texts. Yes, the instructions to the cowboy are there.

Mary is just standing to Edgar's left, looking scared and unsure of herself.

"Relax, Mary. We'll get on to how Edgar almost had Cassie killed in a minute. But first," I look at Edgar, "show me the money."

Edgar does as he's told. He's buying himself time, of course, hoping security will get here.

While he's typing, he looks up at me. He's going to use all his best lies on me, I can see it.

"Lolly, you've got it all wrong," he says, as though there's been an amusing misunderstanding.

"Tell me about the big deal that went bad, Edgar," I say. "Were you using Daddy's money?"

This is a bit of a guess, but I was right with my other suspicions. Edgar was chasing losses only days after Daddy was kidnapped by MI5. It seems too much of a coincidence.

"Lolly," he says, in a weary, authoritative voice. "You're a sweet thing, but you never had any head for money. I'm sure you've conjured up some girlish fantasy about greedy bankers and me stealing your father's wealth, but it's simply not like that. The banking world is actually very boring. There's no story to tell."

I smile. I toss Edgar's phone to Mary. I'm taking a guess on two things here. I'm thinking that she's a bright girl who has been happily facilitating Edgar's shady deals because he pays her well and she's been having sex with her boss.

But I'm also guessing that she knows nothing about professional hitmen and Edgar's willingness to commit murder. I don't think she would be party to that.

I'm right, because the look of shock on her face when she reads the texts is genuine.

"It's not me," Edgar protests to her. "It's some schoolgirl fantasy that she's dreamed up."

I press my feet further into his chest and he grimaces. I almost admire him for maintaining the lie, even when he's been caught red-handed.

"So let me carry on with my fantasy," I say. "Mary, you're a bright girl. I bet *you* do have a good head for money – perhaps you could help me with the details? Is Edgar in financial trouble?"

Mary nods, dumbly.

"Has he been using his clients' money to cover his losses? Clients such as Sir Michael Rosewood, my father?"

Mary nods again, but this time she speaks, too:

"He panicked when he couldn't reach Sir Michael. He'd planned to siphon off money the next time Sir Michael ok'd a transfer. He believed he could make a killing and get the money back before Sir Michael was even aware it had gone."

"So Edgar has been trying to find an alternative ever since? Like Cassie's family?"

Mary is nodding so hard I think her head will roll off.

"He told Cassie he'd leave his wife," I explain. "But then Cassie probably confided in you? She thinks they're planning to buy a house together. I think he's just smooth-talked her into giving him money."

"It's true. I like Cassie," says Mary, shamefacedly. "I never agreed with that."

I'm the last person to comment on other people's morality, but I don't think I'd value Mary as a friend. Maybe she gets a secret kick out of seeing a love rival humiliated? Or am I just overthinking it?

Edgar's mouth is opening and closing, but no words are coming out. He runs a hand nervously through his immaculately coiffed hair.

"And then I showed up. And... what?"

This is the part I don't understand. What did Edgar have against me, to the point that he would try and kill me? I show my frustration by moving one heel up to his neck.

"You could have got your money from Cassie, helped me on my way, and everything would have been fine. So why didn't you?"

"Lolly, please," he puts a hand on my right foot, trying to relieve the pressure on his Adam's apple. He can't shift it an inch. There's a pulse beating in his temple. Large and angry. He's trying to fight back his anger, but he's close to snapping.

"Tell me," I demand. "Edgar, we slept together and then you tried to have me killed. You could have just not called afterwards."

Mary looks even more shocked at that revelation.

Edgar's eyes become soulful.

"Lolly, this was all a terrible mistake. I was trying to help you. I didn't know those men would try and kill you. You know how much I love you! We have something special, don't we? You must have felt that connection last night?"

It's almost comical. I think Edgar has the capacity to believe his own lies. It's virtually a superpower in itself.

"Look me in the eye," he says. He's impassioned, full of outraged innocence. "Do you believe I would do that to you, after what we had last night?"

I should have listened to my father. He told me never to trust anybody. He said he never wanted my heart to get broken.

"You were Daddy's friend. How could you betray him like this?"

And now I see I've pushed the right button. I've unlocked whatever it is inside of him. Something that he would only have spoken out loud in front of my grave. Not that I was going to get a grave. Just a plug hole.

He tries to sit forward in the chair, but I push him back with my foot. His face is flushed and his eyes are like hot coals.

"Betray him? Friend? That's a joke. There's only one person your father trusted and that's his precious princess. Your father's a freak. A total freak of nature, weird mentalist who thank God has finally been locked up. And I hope they throw away the key."

Such is the venom in his voice, I'm stunned. I'm not sure what answer I was expecting, but it wasn't that.

"You think I had a choice in working for him? Do you know what it feels like to lose control of your own mind? To have someone pulling your strings like you're just some kind of puppet?"

The veins are standing out on Edgar's neck. He looks like he's about to have some kind of fit.

"And you," he adds, his eyes flashing with hatred. "Do you think I enjoyed last night? Do you think my skin doesn't crawl at the thought of what I did with Michael's even freakier, lab-experiment, of-a-test-tube, crime-against-nature, daughter?"

I swallow hard.

"The only thing I got a kick out of was knowing that I was hurting your father and hurting you. Oh, and getting paid over a billion pounds for doing it. So thanks for that. I've been working for your father for years, and finally it's paid off."

He's laughing now. I don't know what he thinks he sees in my eyes, but whatever, it prompts him to continue.

"When you came to this building, I thought your father had sent you. I thought he'd found out I'd been taking his money and you were coming to put me in my place. I was scared, Lolly. Petrified at what you were going to do to me."

He looks at Mary. He's suddenly conspiratorial with her.

"You have no idea what it's capable of," he points at me. "It could take on a whole army. That's why MI5 are hunting it."

Why, all of a sudden, am I an 'it'? Mary isn't sure what to believe.

"You have no clue how dangerous it is," presses Edgar. "And her father is ten times worse. You think you're free to go to the shops, or take your boyfriend out to dinner? Think again. Her father could make you do anything he wants. Anything. You can forget free will. They're public enemy numbers one and two. They make Al Qaeda look like the Samaritans."

Mary is just looking at me in bewilderment.

Edgar continues his tirade.

"I never dreamed you could lose your powers. When Cassie told me about you hitting your head and that you were sick, I just had to see it for myself. Had to. Just seeing you, helpless and weak," he snorts. "I loved it. Loved it."

"And I thought I was sick."

"You are, darling. You are. And the others like you. Yes, I know there are others. More freaks." He snorts again. "So when you threw yourself at me like some kind of puppy, and offered me your father's fortune on a plate, I said thank you very much. If anyone bends down low enough, I'll happily kick them in the teeth."

He looks at me, challengingly.

He hands me back the laptop. He'd obviously logged in and then changed his mind and logged out again, because the screen is showing the log-out confirmation.

"I've decided not to give you a penny," he says, defiantly. "The bank accounts still have the money in them and they'll be very useful to me. But I won't give them to an animal like you, not even if you begged me to... and I know you're good at that," he adds.

I sigh. It's a deep sigh and it brings to mind memories of winter evenings at Wentworth Manor, with my father. Daddy has plans for everything. He'd sit with me in the study and tell me all his brilliant ideas. He taught me that people will do anything if they're scared enough. I look at Edgar, and I see his bravado for what it is. Just hysteria, hatred and bile.

He will tell me what I want to know.

I slide my bottom closer to the edge of the desk. I remove my feet from Edgar's chest and place them, either side of him, on the window.

"Let's see who finishes on top, shall we," I say, and kick out at the glass. I'm expecting it to be tough, reinforced, some kind of special safety glass. Maybe it is, but it breaks easily enough.

I lean forward, withdraw my legs, and look Edgar in the eye. His anger has turned to naked fear. I've always experienced a thrill when I execute a target. Daddy knows I enjoy my work and that's why I'm good at it. But not this time. I just feel empty. Sad.

"I'm sorry, Edgar."

Where did that come from? I've never sincerely apologized for anything in my life.

Then I drive my legs forward again and propel Edgar and his chair out of the window. As he disappears through the hole in the frame, I grab his ankles.

Edgar screams, Mary screams, I want to scream.

At this height, the wind is whistling through the office. Mary is hysterical. I can only imagine how many security alarms are going off now. I've got minutes.

Edgar has got the chair wedged between his backside and the glass wall of the building. His arms are waving frantically. His upside-down view of the city should have loosened his tongue.

"What's the password, Edgar?" I shout. "Tell me and I'll let you keep a few million."

I know that he's too scared to even answer me right now. He can barely form a word in his mouth that doesn't begin with 'Arrrrrrrghhhhhhh'.

"Money, Edgar," I say, persuasively. "If you die, you'll never enjoy the pile you've made. You'll never earn another pound, another dollar, another euro. So tell me. What's the password? The word, Edgar? The word is...? The word is...?"

"Narcissus," he screams. "It's narcissus. Please, Lolly. Please."

"Mary, Mary."

Edgar's PA is hysterical, but I need her. I keep shouting her name until she finally looks at me.

"Get a grip," I say, with all the authority I can muster. It does the job. "Take the laptop. Sign him in. Narcissus is the password."

It takes her a full minute to control her fingers enough to sign Edgar in. Curiously, I can see that there are some additional confirmation steps that the bank is asking for. I hadn't considered that, and yet Mary enters them with no problems. I can't believe that Edgar willingly divulged that information, so Mary is obviously a smarter cookie than I've given her credit for.

She's in.

She looks at me. Big eyes, not sure what to think. The scales have dropped regarding Edgar, that's for sure, but I don't think she's ready to see him, or anyone, die.

"Thanks, Edgar," I say, but I make no effort to pull him back up.

"Lolly, for god's sake, please," he cries.

"I don't think you can beg me enough," I reply.

I release my grip on his ankles and he drops, hurtling down and down, bumping off the side of the skyscraper, screaming all the way.

Mary is hyperventilating. She may pass out.

I grab her by the shoulders and try and calm her down, but she backs away and runs out of the door. A pity. I could really have used her help.

I take Edgar's laptop into the adjoining meeting room. As quickly as I can, I change the password and other login details on Edgar's account.

I can see all the bank accounts that Edgar set up for me. I check them against the documentation Edgar provided me with. Looks straightforward enough; I don't think I'll have any more problems. I slip the laptop into my bag.

I look around. My work here is done. I've got what I came for, so it's time to leave before security and the police arrive.

I leave the phones on the table. I recorded the whole conversation with Edgar on the cowboy's phone. I'm happy for anybody to hear Edgar's confession.

I walk calmly out of the door and back towards the lifts. I get in the nearest one and enter.

When I reach the ground floor, there are police swarming all over the place. No one gives me a second glance.

I walk out through the door and into the sunshine.

Chapter 15

Last night I cried again. I hope this won't become a habit. Nothing to worry about. It's only at night, after all. I'm fine during the day.

I have a renewed sense of purpose, I have my powers back, and I have unlimited funds to achieve my goal: rescue my father.

You might be feeling sorry for me, after what Edgar did to me. Or maybe not, after what I did to him. But it's no big deal, you know.

I'm sorry if you wanted to like me. Admit it, you thought I was cute at first. I tugged at your heartstrings with my tale of woe.

But I'm no victim and I'm nobody's fool. Edgar crossed the line when he betrayed Daddy and me. I'm the hero of my story, and you don't want to end up as my villain.

Where Next For Lolly?

If you're missing the messed up Miss Rosewood already, fear not, she'll be returning in the forthcoming full-length Class Heroes novel, *London Belongs to the Alchemist*. Out in 2014.

If you want to be informed about new releases in the Class Heroes series, go to the Class Heroes website and sign up for the Class Heroes newsletter on the website home page.

www.classheroes.com

What Happened... Before?

Class Heroes book 1: *A Class Apart*
Teenage twins James and Samantha Blake are caught up in a
seemingly random terrorist bombing while on a school trip. Many
of their friends are killed. When the twins wake up in hospital,
their lives have changed forever.

The doctors are amazed at the speed with which James and Sam
recover from their injuries and, when the twins begin to exhibit
extraordinary powers, it is obvious that something incredible has
happened.

As James and Sam attempt to overcome their fears and embrace
their new abilities, a series of murders and disappearances start
plaguing the hospital. The twins aren't the only ones with special
abilities and it becomes apparent that someone is coming for them.

Will James and Sam be able to survive the nightmare into which
they have been plunged? Who, or what, is behind the murders at
the hospital? And was that terrorist incident quite so random after
all?

Class Heroes book 2: *What Happened in Witches Wood*
In 1987, 16-year-old Katie Blake died in mysterious circumstances in a stream in Witches Wood.
In 2009, a teenage couple enter the wood one hot, summer night and encounter her ghost.
In 2011, James and Samantha Blake are staying at their grandparents' farmhouse, close to Witches Wood, while they come to terms with their new superpowers.

Those powers are soon put to the test. James comes face-to-face with the ghost of Katie Blake – his long-dead aunt – and discovers that she may be responsible for a number of grisly deaths that have occurred in the wood. Meanwhile, Sam foils an armed robbery in a nearby village and sets in motion a chain of terrible events that threatens the whole family.

Sir Michael Rosewood, owner of the world's largest pharmaceutical firm, knows the secret of their superpowers and has taken a keen interest in the Blake family. But is he friend or foe?

Further Reading

Breaking news on 24/7 Interactive News:
www.247-i-news.com

Acknowledgements

Thanks to my wife Rebecca for all her help, support and professional proofreading services. Thanks also to my Mum, Dad, Brother and, in fact, my entire wonderful family who encouraged me to write, be imaginative and to pursue my dreams.

I love you all very much.

Thanks also to Graham Cleaver for reading through the book, giving me feedback and his seal of approval!

If you want to know more about the Class Heroes books, visit www.classheroes.com

www.ingramcontent.com/pod-product-compliance
Lightning Source LLC
Chambersburg PA
CBHW020642130626
46552CB00003B/1353